THE BLACK COSSACKS

The Black Cossacks Series
Book One

Charles Whiting
writing as
Leo Kessler

SAPERE
BOOKS

THE BLACK COSSACKS

Published by Sapere Books.

24 Trafalgar Road, Ilkley, LS29 8HH

saperebooks.com

ISBN: 978-0-85495-509-1

BOOK ONE: *OPERATION COSSACK*

'The Slavs are to work for us. If we don't need them, they can die... We Germans are the masters — we come first.'

Heinrich Himmler to Baron von Kranz, December 1941.

'Far away my eagles brave are flown
My eagles — Cossacks of the Don.'

Old Cossack Song.

THE KAZAN, SOVIET RUSSIA, FEBRUARY 1942

CHAPTER 1

It was almost night. The darkness was sweeping in rapidly from the west, as if nature were in a hurry to blot out the stark, war-torn landscape of the battlefield below: the firs stripped bare of their foliage by artillery fire so that they looked like gigantic white toothpicks; the burned-out peasant cottages with fire reddened German and Russian tanks lying shattered and abandoned in the churned up fields all around; shell craters, brown against the white of the snow.

But the two pilots had no eyes for the sight below. As the great four-engined Focke-Wulf Condor ploughed steadily eastwards at a speed of 300 kilometres an hour, they concentrated on their green glowing controls. For they both knew that they were over enemy territory. One thousand metres beneath them that apparently abandoned landscape was full of desperate men, hiding in the forests and waiting for the inevitable German attack: men who would kill them both without the slightest compunction.

Another five minutes passed. Twice bright yellow lights flickered angrily on the darkening horizon and shards of red hot steel rapped on the sides of their metal egg shell.

'Flak,' the captain commented.

'Oh, I thought it was rain, skipper,' his companion grunted with a twisted smile, then fell silent as he realised that down below he had picked up the River Don. Like the painful progress of some fatally wounded soldier, its course trailed torturously northwards in the fading light. They would soon be over the planned dropping zone.

The minutes passed leadenly. Although the two pilots, sweating in their thick fur flying overalls, could not see the ground any more, they knew from the briefing that the area was covered in dense, snowbound fir forests: an ideal spot into which they could dump their cargo.

'DZ coming up!' the senior pilot broke the silence suddenly and started to bring the four-engined long distance reconnaissance plane down, lowering the flaps at the same time to reduce his approach speed.

'DZ it is!' his companion grunted, not wasting a word now. In these last nine months since the Führer had attacked the Ivans, the men of the special Zeppelin squadron had made these secret flights far behind the Russian lines often enough. It had become a 'milk run' for them; nevertheless they couldn't afford to be careless. At this range and speed even a Russian blind in one eye could knock the Condor out of the sky. Automatically he flicked on the red warning light to alert the sergeant-dispatcher that they were making their approach run and then started to count off the seconds under his breath. With a bit of luck, they'd be back at their secret base near the Reichsführer HQs in the Ukraine by dawn and he'd be snuggled warmly in bed with his ample breasted auxiliary before the bugle sounded the start of a new day.

The sergeant-dispatcher looked down at the two Russians sleeping on the pile of parachutes at the back of the Condor with unconcealed disgust. Both the big one-armed blond and his short-arsed, dark-eyed companion were dressed in filthy, earth coloured smocks, their knee boots encrusted in mud and their heads shaven to the scalp in the Red Army fashion.

'Popov pigs,' the sergeant muttered to himself as he swayed his way to them, 'happy as swine in shit!' He held on to a strut and aimed a vicious kick at the nearest agent's ribs. '*Davai,*' he yelled above the roar of the plane's straining motors, 'wake up!'

The dark-eyed Russian, who had probably volunteered for this mission to escape from the living death of a Wehrmacht POW camp, woke up immediately. For a brief instant, his Tartar eyes flickered menacingly, then he lowered his gaze. 'What is it, Fritz?'

'Five minutes to DZ,' answered the sergeant-dispatcher. 'You'll be going out for a little walk in space soon.' He grinned unpleasantly. 'So you'd better wake that sleeping beauty over there. Or he'll get the toe of my boot in his cheeky guts smartish. *Davai!*'

The Russian shook his companion. 'Piotr — wake up. We're almost there.'

The one-armed Russian groaned, but did not open his eyes immediately. The Russian called Viktor lit a home-made *Marchoka*, black tobacco wrapped in old newspaper, while the sergeant-dispatcher, fastened himself to the fuselage close to the door by the straps, prior to sending them on their way. Then the steady red light gave way to a winking urgent green.

'All right,' snapped the sergeant, 'jump to it! We're approaching the DZ now.'

The two Russian agents sprang to their feet and began buckling on their twin chutes while the Sergeant flung open the exit door.

An icy wind shot into the plane. 'You first,' he bellowed above the sudden roar and crooked a finger at the Russian with the Tartar's eyes. 'Here.'

The agent, weighed down by his equipment and the two chutes, stumbled to the door and positioned himself there. Down below at a mere four hundred metres, the snowbound countryside was flashing by at a tremendous rate.

'Now you,' he beckoned to blond Piotr.

The Condor was at three hundred and fifty metres, descending rapidly to one hundred and fifty: the minimum jumping height for unskilled men like the two agents. In the ghostly silver light of the moon the Condor's shadow swept ahead of it on the snowy ground like that of some monstrous bird. To their right now, the two Russians could make out the immense stretch of fir forest which would be their hiding place on this first night. Beyond it somewhere in the harsh silver sparkling gloom was their target: the objective for which they had been training so hard in the Ukraine these last few weeks.

'Stand, by!'

The two agents tensed, knees slightly bent against the movement of the plane as it banked. Ahead of them the ground was sliding upwards alarmingly.

The sergeant-dispatcher raised his big hand. The pilot was throttling back violently. The hiss of the wind grew louder.

The fuselage started to tremble with the strain. Holding on tightly with his left hand, the dark-eyed Russian checked his chest chute for the last time.

'*Now!*' the sergeant screamed. The next moment he brought his hand hard down on Viktor's shoulder.

The Russian jumped. The weight of his chutes seemed to snatch him out of the big plane. His arms and legs spread out wildly, he began to drop at a terrifying speed.

The blond Russian took a step forward. 'Are you really sure, Fritz, you want me to go and leave you like this?' he yelled above the howl of the wind, his teeth gleaming in the moonlight.

'*Noew!*' the sergeant roared, dragging the word out. At the same time he aimed a tremendous kick at the cocky Russian's breeches.

The agent shot out of the plane as if he had been catapulted from it, tumbling over and over again as he hurtled towards the ground. For one frightening moment, the sergeant peering over the side with eyes narrowed against the howling wind, thought he wasn't going to make it. Then he heard the loud crack of a chute opening and saw a great white cloud of silk billowing free.

Far above, the sergeant breathed a sigh of relief. The Ivan had recovered from the surprise kick in time, the lucky bastard. But as he began to shoulder the metal door back into place, the sergeant told himself that the two ragged Popovs would be lucky enough if they survived the night in that freezing hell below. Even if they did, they'd be faced with the NKVD, the Russian Secret Police, who were supposed to be everywhere behind the front. Even the most skilled agents that the Zeppelin Squadron had flown into Russia hadn't lasted more than a couple of weeks before the icy cold or the secret police had put a sudden and dramatic end to their clandestine activities.

He shrugged and picked up the intercom. 'Skipper?'

'Yes?'

'They've gone, sir. It's home now for us.'

CHAPTER 2

Dawn. An icy wind swept across the infinite white waste beyond the forest and slashed the watcher's unshaven, red gleaming face with razor-sharp snow crystals. Time and time again he blinked his eyes to force away the tears. Soon, he knew, they would be coming and he could not afford to slacken his watch.

The sickly yellow winter sun slid slowly above the horizon and hung poised there, as if undecided as to whether it should rise any further. Long black shadows raced across the surface of the snow. The watcher held his frozen face up to the light, desperate to catch even the slightest warmth, while his breath fogged the icy air.

Suddenly the frozen watcher caught his breath. From beyond the horizon he had heard a sound like the hum from a hive of swarming bees. He screwed up his eyes to see better as they breasted the horizon, silhouetted starkly against the pale sun.

Prisoners, ten deep, herded along by squat men on tiny ponies, who rode up and down the slow-moving, weary column, cracking their long whips. Hastily he reached down — not taking his gaze off the column for an instant — and shook the other man's shoulder. 'Viktor,' he hissed urgently, 'they're here!'

The Tartar-eyed agent awoke at once. Even under these terrible conditions, he was alert and on his guard as usual. 'Where?'

'There to the west,' Piotr answered, as the other man rolled over next to him to observe the long column of ragged prisoners, shuffling through the snow, urged on by their guards on the shaggy Siberian ponies. 'It's them all right.'

Now they could smell them, although they were at least a verst away. Their stench reminded Piotr of the zoos of his youth. He forced the memory of a better time out of his mind and concentrated on the column as it came closer.

They could see the weary prisoners quite clearly. All wore the same drab uniform — thick felt boots, fur capes and cotton padded blue jackets. But it wasn't the men's uniforms that attracted the watchers' attention; it was the prisoners' sunken eyes, staring fixedly from their emaciated, unshaven faces. To Piotr it seemed that all the world's misery in this terrible winter of 1942 was concentrated in their staggering and stumbling ranks.

An officer, distinguished by his black fur hat and the enormous epaulettes which seemed to weigh down his narrow shoulders, raised himself in the saddle by his stirrups and yelled in a thin voice, 'Column — column halt!'

The prisoners shuffled to a ragged stop and stood there numbly, staring apathetically down at the snow. The little Siberian rapped out a stream of orders in his own language. Quickly the guards urged their shaggy little ponies into the prisoners' ranks, slashing their knouts from side to side, as they divided them up into rough and ready working parties.

'We'd better move back, Viktor,' the one-armed blond giant hissed urgently. 'There's a bunch of the poor devils coming this way.'

Hastily his companion squirmed his way deeper into the cover of the snow heavy trees. Piotr followed a second later, not taking his eyes off the little party of weary prisoners, who were being driven in their direction, heavy logging axes over their thin shoulders.

There was no sound in their part of the forest except for the heavy rhythmic thwack of the two lone prisoners' axes against the tree's thick trunk, and the laboured escape of their breath after each stroke.

Viktor and Piotr were only twenty metres away from them by this time. Advancing slowly and silently like the trained killers they had become over the last weeks, they squirmed gradually closer to their intended victims.

Piotr sized his man up. He could have been about forty-odd, tall and immensely thin, but by the easy way he handled the heavy, two-bladed axe, still a very powerful man, who would know how to defend himself if he felt his life were threatened.

He took a deep breath and flashed a look at Viktor, crouched ten metres away. Viktor nodded. Without wasting another second, they rose simultaneously and pelted forward.

The big man began to lower his axe. He had heard the sound of their feet on the frozen snow. But Piotr's big hand had already sought and found his skinny neck. Piotr exerted pressure. The man's scream was stifled somewhere deep in his throat. He went limp, as if he were already blacking out, his eyes bulging from their sockets, his pale face crimson. Then Piotr made a fatal mistake: he relaxed his grip.

The gaunt prisoner's hands came up, and as if he were swimming the breast stroke, he forced them outwards, breaking Piotr's one handhold. In the next instant he had aimed a vicious chop at Piotr's throat. Piotr threw himself sideways just in time. The prisoner's iron hard hand caught him on the shoulder, but the blow sent him to his knees. Like a wild beast, the prisoner was on him in a flash. Saliva running from his frost-cracked lips, the flaps of his fur hat flopping against his sore-covered cheeks, he fumbled for and found Piotr's ears.

Piotr writhed furiously, trying vainly to break the terrible wrestler hold. Somehow or other he managed to free his one hand from beneath the prisoner. With the last of his strength he rammed his two fingers into the prisoner's wide-open nostrils, and hooking them, ripped upwards.

The man screamed high-pitched and hysterical and fell backwards. Piotr flung himself on him as he writhed from side to side. Clamping bis flapping sleeve across the man's open mouth to stop his screams, he grabbed his shock of grey hair, raised his head and smashed it with all his strength against an outcrop of rock. Five metres away, Viktor strangled the life out of the other man, slowly and pleasurably, his dark Tartar eyes gleaming with almost sexual satisfaction as he did so.

Ten minutes later the two men who had died so violently that morning had been dragged deep into the forest and covered with enough snow to prevent them from being discovered by any wandering guard or hunter. By nightfall the timber wolves would find them anyway and then they would disappear for good. There the killers had pulled off the prisoners' ragged, lice-ridden trousers with the camp numbers on the right thigh. Five minutes after that, the men had picked up the fallen axes and begun hacking away at the tree trunk once more, the blond giant handling his with one hand as if if he had been doing it all his life.

Thus, when the oily skinned Siberian NKVD had come riding up on his shaggy brown pony to inspect what they were doing, there was no sign of any disturbance in the forest glade and the only sound was that of the thwack-thwack of the

16

prisoners' axes striking the wood with the measured pace of men who had all the time in the world to complete their task.

'*Horoscho?*' he enquired.

'*Horoscho,*' they replied in weary unison.

Satisfied that everything was in order, the Siberian raised his knout to his cap with its gleaming, red enamel star in salute and went riding lazily on his way to the next group of woodcutters. The first stage of Operation Cossack had been one hundred per cent successful.

CHAPTER 3

As the long ragged column of exhausted prisoners began to stagger through the great log gate with its red star over the arch, Piotr knew instinctively that he was entering a new and terrible world.

The camp consisted of many hectares of hard-packed earth, shaped in the form of a great hexagon by the three metres high, triple wire fence which surrounded it. As he and Viktor, axes held over their shoulders, came level with the gate, he could see the stork-legged watch towers, in which the Siberians sat, tommy guns slung over their chests, hands resting on the alarm siren. But they weren't the only guards. Between the two outer layers of wire, fierce Alsatian dogs patrolled, saliva dripping from their slack jaws, ready at an instant to go for some unfortunate prisoner's throat or testicles.

'In three devils' name,' Piotr hissed to his companion. 'Look at it — it's like hell on earth, man.'

His companion nodded numbly, his dark eyes watchful as they plodded on to line up with the rest of the prisoners at long wooden tables where surly trustees in dirty aprons and with white masks over their mouths, were thrusting the evening meal at them: Kilka, dry, small salt fish, and *Kipjatok*, half a canteen of hot water to wash them down with.

As they stood there in the freezing air, swallowing the salt fish with difficulty, the two agents furtively surveyed the scene. All around the main square were dirty wooden huts, built on piles so that the guards could poke their metal rods under them to check for escapes or contraband. Between these huts the elderly or the unfit shuffled about on errands like shaven headed skeletons, dragging their felt boots after them as if they weighed a hundredweight. Others squatted on the frozen earth, trying to coax a flame from tiny heaps of twigs and frozen dung so that they could cook pungent white cabbage soups.But the two agents had no eyes for the elderly or the unfit. Their gaze was centred on another and smaller compound at the far end of the concentration camp. This, they knew from their briefing by Intelligence, was the place they had come so far to find: the camp for high-ranking ex-officers and officials now fallen out of favour, who were specially guarded and not allowed on working parties like the rest of the prisoners.

'That's it, Viktor,' hissed Piotr, feeling the salt from the fish bite painfully into the soft flesh at the back of his throat. 'That's where we'll find him, if he's still here.'

Viktor did not answer. His dark eyes were carefully sizing up the prison within a prison.

'It won't be difficult to get into it,' Piotr concluded, spitting out a fish tail. 'The problem will be trying to get out of the place with him —'

His words ended in a grunt of surprise as a heavy shoulder thudded into his. A tall, raw-boned man with clean cut, strongly masculine features had pushed by him and grabbed the discarded fish tail. In one and the same gesture, he lifted it and stuffed it into his mouth.

'You filthy swine,' Viktor snarled, his dark face contorted with disgust and sudden rage. He spat viciously on to the earth at the big man's feet.

'I'm hungry, little brother,' whined the prisoner, licking his lips greedily and eyeing the last of Piotr's *kilka*. 'I am big. I work hard.' He shrugged. 'But the food here is meant for dwarfs.'

Piotr's face relaxed into a good-humoured smile. 'Here,' he handed him the fish, 'here you are little brother.'

To his amazement, the big man bent swiftly and kissed his hard hand. 'Thank you ... thank you, your honour,' he cried fervently, and swallowed the little salt fish in a flash, while Piotr stared at him, more in sorrow than disgust. What a terrible system this must be, he told himself, to reduce human beings to the level of animals.

Then suddenly he heard the thunder of hooves from the far end of the camp. He spun round startled. A squat man on a great white stallion, his long grey officer's cloak streaming out behind him, was galloping furiously towards the main square, bowling over anyone in his way, thrashing his knout from side to side.

'The *Natschalnik*!' cried the big stranger. 'Come on, quick! Run for it!'

Piotr caught one swift glimpse of a high-cheeked face in which were set the dark bottomless eyes of a sadist, then he found himself pushed by the big stranger into the glowing semi-darkness of one of the huts, and heard the door being barricaded hurriedly behind him.

'Phew!' the big man breathed and leaning against the wall, panted: 'That was a close one, brothers! Last week the Commandant had some poor Kalmuck flayed alive because he was too slow in clearing the square after work. They say he's going to make a tobacco pouch out of the poor dead swine's ball sack.'

Piotr looked significantly at Viktor, but the other man's face showed no emotion. His dark gaze was fixed on the glowing interior of the shuttered hut, filled as it was with rough wooden bunks, their feet resting in little tin bowls of water to ward off the bugs, and reaching four storeys high right up to the tin roof. The far end of the hut was packed with bearded old men, obviously unfit for the hard work of the forest, squatting as close as they could to a glowing, pot-bellied stove which provided the only illumination. Some of them were stripped to the waist, searching the seams of their threadbare shirts for lice, but most of them were simply concentrating on keeping warm.

'What do you want in here? This is not your hut, brothers?' demanded a big man, sitting right up to the stove, unwinding his stinking foot-rags.

'I know ... I know, *Starosta*,' said the new comrade hastily, trying to appease the old man by giving him the title of the head-of-barracks. 'But the *Natschalnik* is still out there. You wouldn't want that murderer to catch us, would you?'

The old man puffed out his thick chapped lips. 'I suppose not,' he said finally. 'We don't want to give that swine the pleasure of beating you to a pulp. You can stay if you want... Here,' he pulled a handful of coarse, dry black tobacco from his pocket and offered it to them. '*Marchoka*, but I've got no newspaper, brothers.' 'Don't worry, little Father.' The raw-boned prisoner laughed. 'I saved a little bit of the *Pravda* from the latrine this morning, I thought my arse too good for that lying rag.'

There was slow laughter from the old men, as they parted to let the three newcomers approach the fire to light their homemade cigarettes and settle down to wait for the *Natschalnik* to ride back to his quarters.

In the red glowing gloom, the old men's bearded faces were hollowed out like skulls in the stove's light, their shadows flung on the dripping, bug-infested walls in ever-changing patterns as they listened to the *Starosta's* stories of his years in the prison camps, stretching back as far as the Revolution itself. Camp

500, somewhere beyond the Urals, where he had lived on fish soup and water for a whole year. 'By the Holy Mother of Kazan, that damned fish was born rotten!' he exclaimed in disgust and spat on the stove, making the metal sizzle loudly. The Siberian camp, where they had been dumped in the howling white wilderness with only what they stood up in and ordered by the NKVD guards to start building their own prison. 'And my God,' he cried, 'there wasn't a tree within a hundred square kilometres of the place! We lost every second man that winter, I can tell you, brothers!

'But one thing,' he went on, raising a dirty hand, 'we prisoners must survive. If that Hitler does not free us from those swine in Moscow, we — who survive the war and the camps — will do it ourselves!' His faded old eyes, which had seen so much horror, gazed round their emaciated peasant faces. 'We must live, live every minute till this war is over and that monster Stalin — if he survives — is not expecting any further trouble, especially from within Mother Russia. Then we will give him his trouble — a real bellyful of it!

'Everything we do must be done with the slowest possible movement, not thinking why we do the job or how many hours it takes. When we rise, it must be slow. When we eat, it must be equally slow. When we work, every movement must be made as if with acute pain. We must make time, brothers, in order to survive.'

'And what will you do with your survival, old man?' Viktor asked, not able to restrain his contempt any longer. 'What did you do in the past? Nothing. Now what will you do in the future — the same, I have no doubt.'

The *Starosta* looked at him gravely. 'You are from the Volga, aren't you?' he said finally. 'I can tell the accent. You have lived side by side with the Fritzes for nearly two hundred years. You have acquired some of their impatience with delay. But we of Old Russia are different. We can tolerate much. After all we stood the Czars' tyranny for nearly five hundred years and we've only had Comrade Stalin for a mere twenty. But,' he raised his finger again in warning, 'once our anger is aroused, little brother, we are a terrible people, whose hatred is boundless and can only be extinguished in blood!'

'Talk-talk,' Viktor grunted, his dark face suddenly flushed. 'You of Old Russia always talk and never act.'

'No, little brother,' interrupted the raw-boned man. 'I didn't just talk. I killed a NKVD sergeant with these hands,' he looked down at his big calloused paws, as if he could still see the murdered man's blood on them. 'That is why I am in this hellhole.'

Piotr flashed a warning look at his fellow agent. Viktor would be getting himself in trouble if he didn't keep his big mouth shut.

But his look of warning was unnecessary.

At that very moment, there was a tremendous kick at the door of the hut and a gruff voice demanded: 'Open this shitty door, or we'll kick it down on you!'

The *Starosta's* face blanched. 'Holy Mother of Kazan.'

'Who is it?' Piotr asked hastily. 'The *Natschalnik*.'

The raw-boned prisoner gulped. 'No,' he said, 'worse. It's Zariza's women.'

At that moment half a dozen sturdy shoulders were flung against the door. Once. Twice. The bar holding it splintered and cracked in half. The door flew open and into the room erupted a horde of screaming women the like of which Piotr had never seen before. Some of them were obviously gravely undernourished. Their arms were wasted and bony, their hands filthy claws, their hair, without lustre, hung down their thin faces, leaden with the blue tint of want.

Others were raw-boned, heavy bosomed peasant women in their thirties, with fists like hams, their hair cropped as short as any man's, their well-fed faces heavy chinned and aggressive. But all of them were bright-eyed and hysterical as they poured through the door, as if they had been drinking heavily or taking drugs.

For a moment they crouched like famished timber wolves, while the old men cowered back against the wall, fear distorting their worn faces. Then a gruff voice commanded: 'All right, you sows — get out of my way!'

A huge woman with cropped jet-black hair and dark flashing gypsy eyes forced a path through the excited women and faced them, booted feet planted squarely apart like a man. Deliberately she took the black cigar she was puffing out of her mouth and threw back the grey officer's cloak she was wearing.

Piotr gasped. The huge woman was naked to the waist. Pendulous breasts, tattooed obscenely in blue and with startling red nipples, hung down to her broad, iron-buckled man's belt.

She spat on the floor slowly and contemptuously. 'A fine bunch of soft, short pricks,' she grunted in a deep bass. 'Not one of the old bastards could get it up even if you kept them in a whore-house for a month of Sundays. We're wasting our time here. I —'

'Katya,' a skinny blonde at her side tugged at her muscular arm and nodded at the tall raw-boned prisoner who had stolen Piotr's fish. 'That one, Katya. Look at his shoulders — they're bent, that's always a good sign. And the size of his nose, that's another.' The blonde closed one eye significantly. 'He'll be all right, or I'll be screwed stupid. Perhaps he'll give our Zariza pleasure.'

Katya pushed her away impatiently while she sized up the man. Then she clicked her fingers. Two of the peasant-looking women moved forward. Knives gleamed suddenly in their ham like fists.

The raw-boned man backed away, his hands stretched out to ward them off. 'No,' he protested. 'Don't pick on me ... I'll be no good. I don't get enough to eat ... I have to work too much. Zariza would never like what —'

The words died somewhere in his throat as one of the women lunged forward. The blade of her knife flashed wickedly in the ruddy half-light, slicing the man's belt with one swift stroke. Again Katya clicked her fingers. The women swarmed forward and surrounded him. The low ceilinged room was filled with the tremulous waves of their shrill excited laughter as they uncovered his body, ripping and tearing at his clothing. One of them tripped him up. He tried to keep his balance but failed and stumbled to the floor. They swarmed over him, their eyes greedy and filled with lust, as they tore away the last shred of his clothing.

Piotr swallowed hard, sickened by this display of naked impersonal lust. Yet all the same, he told himself, he must not interfere. Whoever they were, they were dangerous, highly dangerous. He could see that from the terrified look of the poor bastard spread-eagled on the dirty floor and that on the faces of the old men. These were not women of the kind he knew; they were dumb, vicious animals.

Katya ran her gypsy eyes slowly down the length of her victim's lean, naked body until she stopped at the genitals. Deliberately she placed her muddy boot on his chest and rolled her cigar into the corner of her broad mouth, before asking: 'You're not queer, man, are you?'

'No, but I'm no good for Za —'

His protest ended in a stifled gurgle of pain as she stamped her boot down on his exposed throat. 'Shut your dirty man's mouth,' she snarled. 'You were asked a question, prick. Answer it — that's all, understood.'

Slowly she bent, her naked breasts dangling on to his sweat-streaked chest and while Piotr and the rest watched in fascinated horror, she reached out a dirty paw and seized the trapped man's genitals.

For a long moment she toyed with them, running her fingers through the surrounding hair like a peasant woman trying to judge the weight of a goose at a country market. Then she straightened up again puffing hard on her cigar and wiping her fingers on the seat of her trousers, as if they were disgustingly dirty.

'He'll do,' she announced. 'We'll take him.'

'No,' the man screamed. 'Please not me!'

The woman did not hear. Throwing her cloak across her naked breasts, she turned and strode imperiously to the door. Half a dozen of the peasant women lifted the prisoner. He tried to struggle, but one of the women brought her hand down in a vicious chop against his throat. The man screamed, then his head lolled to one side and his struggles ceased.

An instant later they had gone, bearing their unconscious burden with them into the freezing darkness while the assembled men stared at the open door swinging softly to and fro in the wind.

CHAPTER 4

The other prisoners found the man the women had kidnapped at dawn. He was dead.

He was framed in a star of his own blood, sprawled out face down on the parade ground, his naked body already stiffening in the cold dawn air. The bent-shouldered prisoners, assembling for the day's work, stared numbly at the dead body while the NKVD guards doubled forward in their heavy boots to examine the corpse. The first of them dug his boot under the body and heaved it over. There was a shocked gasp from the prisoners. The body had been horribly mutilated.

'Oh, my God!' breathed Piotr in horrified revulsion, 'look what they did to him!'

'The barbaric swine,' Viktor snarled, his dark eyes eating up the scene of horror which shocked even the hard-bitten Siberian guards.

'*Bitches*, you mean,' the *Starosta* corrected him softly. 'Zariza's women, they did it.'

'But why?'

The old man's answer was interrupted by a clatter of horse's hooves from the direction of the special camp.

'*The Natschalnik*!' a sergeant yelled urgently.

The NKVD guards slashed their knouts to left and right, forcing the prisoners into ragged lines, as the *Natschalnik* reined his white horse to a stop in a flurry of snow.

For the first time Piotr saw the Camp Commandant clearly, and he did not like what he saw. The officer was a small Siberian like the rest of the guards. But whereas their dark eyes were those of unthinking peasants, his were those of a sadist, the torturer, the slow killer. For a moment he poised there on the back of his big white horse, staring down at the naked body. Then with the ease of the born rider, he bent down and dug his knout into the gory mess of the man's genitals.

'Get rid of him,' he ordered in a curiously high-pitched voice, 'at once!' As if to emphasise his command, he swung the knout at the sergeant.

As the Commandant swung his horse round and galloped off the way he had come, prisoners hurried forward to drag away the mutilated body. A minute later it had been flung to one side, as if it were a log of wood.

Following the rest of the prisoners as they shuffled towards the log gate for another day's back-breaking work in the forest, Piotr whispered to his companion: 'Viktor, what in three devils' name, have we let ourselves in for here? If we ever fall into that man's hands — or worse — those women's, we will be eternally grateful to God if we're allowed to die quickly.'

Viktor spat bitterly into the snow. He didn't say anything, but his dark Tartar eyes revealed the depths of his own fears.

When they staggered into the old men's hut that evening, frozen and worn out, their bodies aching all over, they were greeted by the savoury smell of meat roasting. Their weariness vanished like magic, their stomachs rumbling noisily at the prospect of hot food.

At the glowing stove, the *Starosta* looked up from his steaming pot, his bearded face red from the heat, his eyes glowing in pleasurable anticipation, and beckoned to them to come closer. 'Have you eaten?'

Piotr, too exhausted to speak, shook his head, and Viktor, his eyes fixed greedily on the pot's contents, added wearily: 'Just the *Kilka*.'

'*Kilka!*' the old man grimaced. 'One minute — and you can have a piece of meat each.'

Sixty seconds later they were devouring the meat ravenously, the grease dripping down their unshaven chins unheeded, gasping as the hot meat stung their tongues.

Viktor wiped the grease off his chin. 'What kind of meat was that, *Starosta*? It tasted excellent.'

The Starosta's faded eyes sparkled suddenly. 'Roof-hare.'

'Roof-hare?'

'Yes, that's right, my smart lad from the Volga,' straight from the guards' own kitchen. It was that big fat juicy ginger cat that hunted the rats in the storeroom!' He threw back his bearded chin and roared with laughter at their looks of shock and surprise.

Then, as they squatted on the floor smoking the foul-smelling black *Marchoka*, stomachs pleasantly full, weariness forgotten, he told them about Zariza's women.

'They're the *Blatnajas*,' he explained slowly, puffing hard at the cigarette to keep it alight. 'There've been women like that in every camp I've ever been in. Murdering, thieving, whoring to keep themselves alive when everyone else is dying all around them.' He shrugged expressively. 'They are, if you like, the system within the system. Poor little worms like ourselves try to survive individually. They have learned that the only way to survive in these hells is to band together — and that is their strength. If you try to tackle one of them, you have the whole thieving whoring pack of 'em on to you. Yes, during the day the *Natschalnik* might rule this camp, but after dark, it belongs to the *Blatnajas*.' He spat reflectively against the glowing side of the stove.

'But doesn't he know?' Piotr protested. 'I mean why doesn't the *Natschalnik* stop it? Why does he let them get away with it?'

The old man looked at him curiously. 'You don't know much about the camps do you? You must be new here. I thought everybody here knew what kind of hold Zariza has over the *Natschalnik.*'

Viktor flashed Piotr a warning look. 'We have been just sent here,' he explained hastily. 'We are deserters from the front.'

'Oh, I see. Well, Zariza was once the mistress of the great man himself.' He chuckled sourly. 'No less than our little Father Lavrenti Pavlovich Beria.'

'*Beria!*'

The old man was pleased with the effect he had achieved. 'Yes, the man who is responsible for our all being in this living hell. Beria, the head of the NKVD.'

'But how did this — er — Zariza come to be associated with such a high animal?' Piotr asked, watching the flames from the oven weave a trembling pattern across the old man's face.

'Because Zariza is the greatest whore Mother Russia has produced since the days of the Great Catherine. Before Beria met her, he was normal — or as normal as any of those swine in the Kremlin can ever be. Everyone in Moscow in those days knew that it was Zariza who cured him of his impotency. It was she who introduced him to his devilish perversions after all.'

'Impotency — perversions?' Piotr asked.

'It was an open secret among those who lived in Moscow before the war. Many times I have seen this big black German car cruising the streets, looking for fresh blood. You see the Zariza taught him to like very young girls. And that was only one of the nasty tricks she taught that monster so that he could satisfy his filthy lust. There were others — much worse.' He narrowed his eyes darkly. 'If what I heard in Moscow in those days is true, the two of them were devils in human form.'

'But if she had such a hold over Beria?' Viktor said, 'how did she land in this place, *Starosta*?'

'Well now, that's a little difficult to explain,' he replied. 'Naturally he no longer found her sexually attractive, although she is insatiable — you saw what happened to that poor fellow this morning because he couldn't satisfy her. But she was too old for him. Yet all the same, Beria must have had it at the back of his mind that she had cured his impotency once — he might need her again. Those Georgians — Stalin and Beria — are superstitious folk, you know. So when he decided to get rid of her, he put her inside this camp, instead of liquidating her in case he ever needed her expert services again.

'The *Natschalnik* treats her with kid gloves. If the Little Father in Moscow ever does need her once more, the *Natschalnik*, sadist that he is, knows he wouldn't survive long if she reported to Beria that she had been ill-treated here in the camp. Thus she has a hut to herself in the inner camp with the big animals —'

Viktor flashed a quick look at Piotr, but the old man did not notice. 'And her *Blatnajas* can come and go as they wish, bringing new lovers for her. And if they don't satisfy her, well you saw what that poor fellow looked like this morning.'

'You mean that is why he was murdered?' Viktor asked.

The *Starosta* nodded sombrely. 'Yes. That one is as insatiable as the Great Catherine herself. She must have men — men like this,' he held his work-hardened hands apart. 'And if they don't satisfy her, then —' He drew a line across his throat, 'they die.'

That night, as they lay in their lice-ridden wooden bunks, with their exhausted fellow prisoners snoring heavily all around them, Piotr reached out carefully and touched Viktor's shoulder.

'Are you awake?' he whispered.

Viktor, his head resting on his hands, folded underneath his head, looked up at him in the fading ruddy light of the dying stove. 'Yes, I'm awake. But when I realise what's facing us out there in the forest tomorrow, I know I should be long asleep.'

'I know, I know,' Piotr agreed. 'But Viktor, we must contact him tomorrow before those harpies of Zariza or that *Na schalnik* come looking for us. Do you agree?'

Viktor hesitated only one moment before he whispered: 'All right, Piotr, tomorrow it is.'

CHAPTER 5

Their entrance into the special camp reserved for important opponents of the Soviet Regime, turned out to be surprisingly easy.

Once the two agents had dodged the morning roll-call for the working parties, they found they could move around the outer camp quite freely without anyone taking much notice of them. The place was full of elderly men going about their routine duties, and weary prisoners waiting in a long line to see the fat Jewish woman MO, whose remedies for their manifold ills and diseases were confined to aspirin, hot water and enemas. Thus as they made their way to the central camp, buckets clutched in their hands as camouflage, no one paid the slightest attention to them or queried why two apparently fit young men should not be outside in the forest with the working parties.

With apparent nonchalance, they paced out the perimeter of the place. Almost immediately they dismissed the main gate as a means of entrance. It was guarded by a young NKVD corporal who had the look of a man out for swift promotion. He was too keen — he might ask awkward questions. In the soft warm rain, the first sign of coming spring, they trudged on. Then Piotr spotted it. A great dripping wooden bucket on wheels, its sides encrusted with lime, and exuding an appalling stench. 'That's it,' he exclaimed excitedly. 'The latrine wagon!'

Viktor gagged and pinched the end of his nose in a vain attempt to ward off the evil smell. 'You don't have to tell me,' he said thickly, 'you can smell the damn thing a verst away.'

'Ah, but that is a very special shit cart,' Piotr said cheerfully. 'That particular one is going to get us inside there. In one second flat, Viktor, you are going to become a humble shit shoveller.' Piotr gripped the handle with his big hand and began to trundle the nauseating wagon towards one of the side gates.

'But won't they spot we're not the regular men?' Viktor protested.

'That's a chance we'll have to take,' Piotr answered. 'In this kind of weather, most sentries are busy keeping their heads dry. Besides they'll be most likely watching for people trying to get *out* of the place, not *into* it.'

'Let's hope you're right.'

Piotr was. The bored Siberian guard, sheltering in his striped sentry box, did not even look up as they trudged by through the mud. He raised his free hand automatically to his nose to shut out the stench but kept his gaze fixed on the toes of his dirty boots. Five minutes later they had dumped it behind a hut and begun their exploration of the special camp.

The spring rain had driven the special prisoners from the compound into their huts. Now as they peered through the cracked, dirty windows, the two agents could see the Soviet Union's 'special guests', both men and women, trying to kill another long day. Some were already cooking their midday meal, soups of evil-smelling white cabbage and indescribable dark lumps of what might have been meat. Others were hunched deep in thought over games of chess, long Russian cigarettes clenched in their fingers, glasses of herbal tea at their side, while a few simply slumped on their bunks and stared apathetically into space.

'Just look at them, Viktor,' Piotr whispered, 'once they were the police, the judges, the generals, the great men's mistresses with power of life and death over thousands. Now they can't even be sure if they'll live to eat their next meal. It's a commentary on human existence, isn't it?'

'Don't be so damn romantic, Piotr. Concentrate on finding the man we're looking for. It's dangerous in here, you know.'

In silence they continued their search for the man whose face they had studied on half a hundred faded photographs ever since Operation Cossack had been agreed upon. It was raining hard and the long-frozen winter earth was beginning to thaw. They ploughed their way grimly through the thick mud, necks buried in the collars of their dripping smocks, staring through each new window in the hope that they would see his unmistakable features behind it. But the man seemed to be nowhere.

They stopped and sheltered for a moment under the dripping eaves of one of the huts lining the main square, now a sea of mud. 'Do you really think he is here?' Viktor asked gloomily.

'Our people were one hundred per cent positive,' Piotr answered, wiping the rain from his face. 'Goddamit, Viktor, he's got to be!'

'But what happens when we reveal our identity to him, Piotr? I mean what if he betrays us to the guards? Can we trust him?'

Piotr looked up and down the muddy street hastily. There was no one in sight. Swiftly he raised his right foot and felt for the catch which opened the carefully concealed spring in the heel. Viktor watched him puzzled. Then the heel swung back to reveal the little pistol hidden there in the hollow. 'The latest thing developed by our *Abwehr* people,' Piotr explained, quickly fitting the battery. 'I know it doesn't look much, but it'll kill a man at ten metres — without a sound.' He gave it a swift check and slipped it in the pocket of his blouse. 'You can be sure of one thing, Viktor. The moment he opens his mouth to yell for the guards, he's a dead man.'

Five minutes later, they found him. The man they had come so far to contact was standing with his back to them in the camp's 'House of Culture', staring at the two fly-blown, garlanded portraits of Lenin and Stalin, which were the dreary room's sole attempt at 'culture'.

'It's him!' Piotr whispered urgently. 'There can be no mistake. Look at his height and that *Cherkesska*. No one else but a Cossack would dare wear that.'

Viktor nodded. Piotr was right. The tall, erect man, clad in the knee-length, wide-frocked black coat could be only one person — Hetman Alexei.

For a moment Piotr hesitated. He licked suddenly dry lips. After all these long weeks of discussion, preparation, danger, he was suddenly at a loss. How did he start? What if Viktor had guessed right and the Hetman turned out to be a loyal Soviet citizen in spite of the way he had been treated? What then?

Nervously he gripped the tiny pistol with fingers that were wet with sweat. He stared at the Hetman's broad muscular back through the open door, his mind racing frantically, the pouring rain unheeded, as he considered how he should make his approach.

But in the end it wasn't the agent who spoke first. 'Well,' a voice, cold, disciplined, well-used to giving orders, broke the uneasy silence, 'what do you two want from me?'

Piotr flashed a look of wonder at Viktor.

The Hetman answered the unspoken question for him. 'The glass,' he said easily. 'I can see you in the glass.' Then he turned to meet them.

Hetman Alexei was an impressive sight. Taller than Piotr, his face, framed by black curly hair, was harshly handsome and masterful, marred only by the trace of bitterness around the mouth. But despite that, he looked immensely tough and self-assured. The rakish tilt of his fur cap on the side of his head, the slant of his long Russian cigarette, the immaculate flamboyant coat — all indicated a man who knew precisely the worth of everything and everybody: a man who looked every inch a Cossack general, a man used to command.

For a long moment he stared silently at the two agents, as if they were two new recruits from the country and he were a young captain of cavalry again. 'Well,' he barked finally, apparently satisfied, 'what do you two shit-shovellers want from me? I've been watching you prowl around the camp these last ten minutes like two lost foals looking for the mare?' His lean cleanly-shaven jaw hardened. 'Are you Zariza's people, eh?' His look indicated what he thought of the *Blatnajas*.

'No, Hetman,' Piotr stuttered, made uneasy by the savage strength of the man which he could feel like an electric shock wave.

'*Hetman!*' Alexei echoed, his face suddenly thoughtful. 'It's a long time since I heard that title, brother. These days I think of myself as Number A-4599.' He touched the patch on his riding breeches. Then his voice grew harsh, almost overbearing. 'All right,' he snapped, 'you seem to know who I am. Now then who are you?'

The two agents clicked their heels together in the German fashion. '*Major Baron Peter von Kranz,*' Piotr snapped. '*Zu Befehl!*'

Next to him Viktor rapped, '*Obersturmbannführer Viktor Teufel, Herr Hetman!*'

Hetman Alexei of the Don Cossacks lost his fabled composure. 'Fritzes,' he breathed incredulously, Tritzes here — in this place!'

BERLIN, DECEMBER 1941

CHAPTER 1

For Baron Peter von Kranz Operation Cossack (as it came to be called later) had started on the morning of December 11th, 1941.

At ten o'clock precisely on that frosty morning, his grey Wehrmacht staff car drew up outside the forbidding Bendlerstrasse Headquarters of the Greater German Army. Ordering the driver to ignore the parking prohibition and wait, he whispered a few hurried words of Russian to his strange passenger, then clattered up the white frozen steps past the rigid sentries of the Berlin Guards Battalion.

Oberst von Tresckow, Kluge's Chief of Operations was waiting for him on the second floor, his red face beaming with pleasure, hand already stretched out in welcome. 'Good to see you again, Peter! Glad to have you back in harness once more.'

'They can't get rid of weeds, Oberst,' Peter replied using the soldiers' expression.

Colonel von Tresckow had been von Kranz's regimental commander when Piotr had lost his arm at the River Bug assault crossing the previous summer, at the start of the great offensive against Russia. He ran his eyes up and down his onetime subordinate's immaculate uniform, complete with the black wound medal and black and white Knight's Cross. 'You look very well, Peter, very well indeed. And the arm?'

The younger officer shrugged. 'All right, I suppose, Colonel. Sometimes I get a hell of an itch in the fingers — and then find that they're no longer there,' he laughed ruefully. 'Otherwise everything's in butter.'

'Good, good. It's a shame, but well — let's say you've earned your piece of tin,' he indicated the medal round von Kranz's neck, as he ushered him into the office. 'Now you can settle into a nice comfortable slot on the Field Marshal's staff with a clear conscience. You've done your bit. Heaven, arse and twine — that you have, and paid your price in flesh and blood for it. Now then, what's the problem?' He pushed across the box of cigars. 'I thought you'd jump at the idea of becoming my intelligence officer — you with your Russian background.'

Von Kranz refused the offer of the cigars. 'That's exactly it, Colonel. I don't want to spend the rest of the war as a base stallion, getting a fat rear and probably piles to boot. I want —'

'Yes, do tell us what you want, Major.'

The two officers swung round. Framed at the door of the inner office stood Field Marshal Hans von Kluge, the new commander of the troops in Russia, 'clever Hans' himself, immaculate, despite his addiction to expensive cognac and Berlin society women.

'Tresckow,' he said, 'what in three devils' name are we going to do about the winter oil situation? The General Quartermaster has just been on the phone, but he can't promise me anything. And out there,' with an angry wave of his elegant hand he indicated the east, 'there isn't a drop of winter grease for field glass lenses, trench telescopes, gunsights. If the optics freeze over, our men are blinded, our guns useless.'

'It is being taken care of, Generalfeldmarschall,' von Tresckow snapped. 'Fifty tons, courtesy Admiral Dönitz, are already on their way.'

'Does the Big Lion know he has been so courteous?' von Kluge asked.

'Not yet, sir. And when he does, it'll be too late.'

Von Kluge allowed himself a tired smile and turned his attention to Kranz again. 'Now then young man what's this all about? You'd better come in here and tell me.'

'Well sir,' von Kranz began, a little nervous at the prospect of briefing the Army Commander in the East, 'as you know, Colonel-General von Manstein's Eleventh Army is to have priority for the coming summer offensive to conquer the Caucasus and capture the Russian oilfields with the left flank of his Eleventh attacking east as far as Stalingrad on the River Don?'

'Yes, yes, I know. The Führer's got that damned Russian oil on the brain. Go on.'

'Well, sir, when the Colonel-General starts his offensive, I wonder if you know what troops will be defending the Army's northern flank?'

Von Kluge shook his head a little irritably. 'Look, young man, I've been in command exactly forty-eight hours and already I'm up to my neck with a thousand and one problems, from what size contraceptives the troops are to be supplied in the rear areas to whether camp cinemas should show captured Tommy musicals. No, I don't know. Tell me — and why.'

'Magyars and Italians, sir.'

'Oh, not the damned Macaronis!' groaned von Kluge.

'Yes, sir. And that's why I'm here. As we all know our Italian allies have not proved themselves the most reliable of soldiers.'

Next to him, von Tresckow chuckled. 'I believe in the Desert they have been taking off their boots so that they can run faster.'

Von Kluge froze him with an icy look. 'All right, young man, get on with it.'

'Well, sir, how can we hold such a vast front with troops of that type. We need a much more aggressive, reliable type.' He hesitated momentarily. 'What we need — is Russians, sir.'

'I've heard that suggestion before.' He nodded at Tresckow. 'This dear Colonel's favourite Russian Liberation Army. No, no, Major von Kranz, the Führer wouldn't ever buy that. You know his thoughts on the Russians, I'm sure.'

'Yessir. I know, sir. But we must convince the Führer that we need the Russians — at least, those who are prepared to fight for their freedom from the Kremlin's domination. You see, sir, I am a Baltic German. My forefathers served the Russian state loyally for over two centuries. It was only when Imperial Russia fell apart and the Reds took over that we transferred our loyalty to Germany. But there were others, who never stopped resisting the Reds even when the rest of the world thought Bolshevism had finally triumphed.'

'And who are these paragons of virtue and stubbornness?' von Kluge asked drily.

Von Kranz ignored the irony. 'The Cossacks, sir, *the Cossacks!* And some of them are still resisting to this very day. Sir, if you'll bear with me for a couple of minutes, I should like to show you something.'

The man whom the young Major and his driver bore in would have been a giant if he had been able to walk upright. His head and face were a mass of grey hair and he had a splendid beard which covered a massive chest. An enormous man in every sense — save that he was legless.

The two men placed him carefully on a chair, while von Kluge stared at them as if they had gone out of their minds. 'What ... who is this?' he finally managed to stutter.

'*Herr Generalfeldmarschall*, may I introduce you to the last Field Hetman of the Don Cossacks, General Kulakov!' On the chair the grotesque figure nodded his magnificent bearded head solemnly in recognition of his name.

'But General Kulakov — *the* General Kulakov was killed at the end of the Russian Civil War,' von Kluge objected. 'I know — I had served on the Russian front in '18 and I followed the course of the White battles against the Bolsheviks in the years that followed.'

Von Kranz allowed himself a small smile of triumph. 'I know, sir, that is what everyone else thought too. But it wasn't so. After Vorishilov's Red Cavalry defeated the White Cossacks on the Don in '21, the General went into hiding with a few followers in the Caucasus Mountains. He had been very badly wounded in the fighting as you can see — and couldn't escape across the Black Sea to Turkey as a lot of them did. He remained behind, recovered and became the focal point for any dissident Cossack who could not stand the Red oppression.'

'Do you mean to tell me that … that man has been hiding since the Revolution?'

'And several thousand more with him, sir. You see, sir, when I was still recuperating in Poland from my wound, I used to ride out every morning to strengthen my remaining arm. One morning I bumped into a wandering group of horsemen dressed in a uniform I only remembered from the Russian illustrated papers of my youth. But at that moment, it wasn't their uniform that interested me, it was the fact that the horsemen were wandering about two hundred kilometres behind the front — armed with rifles and sabres. I was round like a shot and back to the nearest German Field Gendarmerie post. Within the hour the chain-dogs had rounded them up and it was then I first met General Kulakov here.'

'You mean, they were Cossacks bringing him over to our lines?' von Kluge asked, intrigued despite himself.

'Yessir. After twenty years in hiding they had brought him out of the mountains, crossed the length of the Caucasus, penetrated our front in the Crimea without being detected and were on their way to Berlin. The General had the idea that he would find the Führer there and convince him to send a commander to rally the Don Cossacks in a great revolt against the Bolsheviks. He might not have been too well informed about the habits of our Führer, Herr Generalfeldmarschall, but he'd already covered over a thousand kilometres, wounded but undetected, and if it hadn't have been for my early morning ride last September, he might well have made Berlin by now —'

Von Kluge held up his hand for quiet, his keen eyes fixed on the mutilated Russian's face, his weariness gone. 'Clever Hans' was no fool. He knew that his predecessor von Bock had been granted indefinite 'sick leave' because he had failed to deliver Moscow, 'the Soviet Head' to the Führer. Now he, von Kluge, was to capture the 'Soviets' guts', the Don industrial basin and the Caucasian oil on the basis of a plan drawn up by Adolf Hitler. But he wasn't happy with that plan. The Wehrmacht had suffered tremendous losses trying to take Moscow — perhaps a million dead and seriously wounded. Where now was he to find the men to supply Manstein's Army with the muscle it needed to attack south-east, unless he drained the rest of the front of reserves?

Young von Kranz was a fool to think that the Führer would ever tolerate the establishment of a Russian Liberation Army. For Hitler the Russians were nothing better than sub-human creatures, fit only to be slaves for the German master race. He would never allow German weapons in Russian hands. No, there could be no question of Russian renegades from the millions of Red Army prisoners in German hands taking their place in the line alongside German soldiers.

He sucked his teeth and stared again at the Cossack general who had travelled so far to appeal to a Führer whose attitude to the Russian people was simply one of blind hate. The man was impressive, very impressive indeed. The thought that there might well be several thousand more Cossacks just like him, sworn enemies of the Bolsheviks and born fighters, located in a strategically vital position right behind the Russian southern front began to intrigue him. What if such men, already armed and at the command of one of their own leaders, attacked the Russian rear on the same day that Manstein launched his great offensive? It might just be the one stroke that would throw the Ivans off guard. If it succeeded, then he would tell the Führer what he had done in the hope that 'success solves all problems'; if it failed, no-one would need to know.

He broke the heavy silence. 'Von Kranz, I appreciate that you and Colonel von Tresckow are aiming at higher things. But my dear Major, in this business — and especially if we poor soldiers are plagued with political masters such as we have — one has to learn to walk before one can run. Remember the old Prussian motto *Mehr sein als scheinen*. There can be no thought of a Russian Liberation Army —'

Von Kranz opened his mouth to protest, but the Field Marshal waved him to silence.

'*Just now*, I was going to say,' he added softly. 'However, we *can* use General Kulakov's Cossacks for another operation I have in mind. This is what I suggest...'

CHAPTER 2

'*Reichsführer!*'

Heinrich Himmler, the black-clad head of the SS, looked up from his papers, frowning severely as usual. 'Yes Teufel?'

Obersturmbannführer Viktor Teufel cleared his throat formally. 'Baron von Kranz of Field Marshal von Kluge's staff,' he announced. 'You recall his proposal, sir?'

The most feared man in Europe nodded and looked out of the window momentarily into the courtyard of the Gestapo HQ, as if he had still not made up his mind, whether he should receive the staff officer. He knew the people at the Bendlerstrasse; they were always full of crazy schemes directly opposed to National Socialist policy. Outside the snow was coming down in a merciless white fury, as if God had decided he would blot out this miserable war-torn world for good. 'All right, Teufel,' he said, 'show him in.'

At the door, Baron von Kranz, immaculate as ever, snapped to attention, his grey-gloved hand raised to the gleaming peak of his cap. 'Major von Kranz, zu Befehl, Reichsführer!'

For a moment Himmler eyed Kranz's handsome, good-humoured face, his dark eyes resting enviously on the Knight's Cross, the decoration he coveted more than anything else in the world. Then he said, 'I see you got your piece of tin, Major.'

'Yes Reichsführer. At the price of one missing flipper,' he indicated his empty sleeve.

'All right Major,' Himmler said, sitting back in his carved high-backed chair and pressing his thin fingers together. 'You have exactly fifteen minutes to state your cause. I am due back at my HQ in the Ukraine this evening and I have a lot to do by then.'

But if he had expected Major von Kranz to be disconcerted by his standard opening gambit, designed to put the traditional Wehrmacht officer in his place, he was disappointed. Instead von Kranz looked at the dark-haired officer with the white armband of the *Liebstandarte Adolf Hitler* on his right sleeve.

'You need not worry, Major,' Himmler said, catching the direction of his gaze. 'Teufel is in on this — he's my expert on Russian affairs. He was born on the Volga — an ethnic German. Lived there until he was fifteen — speaks the language fluently.'

Teufel's face remained impassive, while von Kranz stared at his dark features, with the slanting un-Aryan eyes.

'As you know, sir, since the start of *Barbarossa*, we have lost some one and a half million German soldiers, dead and seriously wounded.'

'They will be replaced, Major, never fear.'

'We cannot afford such terrible losses, sir. What are we to do, therefore? We must find other means of helping the Führer to defeat the enemy. We must try to defeat him from within. As you know, there are large groups of people within the Soviet Union who are completely disillusioned and dissatisfied with the Communist regime and are eager and willing to help us to overthrow it. If you recall last autumn, Reichsführer, when we marched into the Ukraine, thousands welcomed us as liberators and virtually every line unit has ex-Russian prisoners working in its rear echelon. Indeed last month, more than one hard pressed unit, actually put ex-Reds into the firing line when the going got too tough — and they didn't hesitate to fire upon their own —'

'Major von Kranz,' Himmler interrupted the enthusiastic flow of words severely. 'I think you as a National Socialist officer should know the Führer's and my own attitude to the Russians. They are little better than animals — sub-humans. The Slavs are to work for us. If we don't need them, they can die. Those who survive should get no more food than necessary. They may abort and use contraception — the more the better. As for education,' he shrugged, 'it's enough if they can count up to one hundred. Religion we'll leave to them as a harmless diversion. And above all they can have no political or military aims.' He poked a skinny white finger at his own thin chest, bare of any decoration save the Sports Medal. 'We Germans are the masters — we come first!'

'But Reichsführer,' von Kranz protested hotly. 'I am a Baltic German. My family has lived among the Slavs for hundreds of years. We know them and their great potential. Why ignore the vast human resources that lie there for our use?' He pulled himself together quickly and started on the argument that von Tresckow had advised him to use with the racialist head of the SS. 'Of course, we all know the Führer's and the Party's attitude to the Slavs, but can't we throw our principles or racial purity overboard in this our time of need? After the war is over and we have beaten them, we shall be able to think more clearly about the Aryan dogma. But first we must *beat* them. For the time being, let us put these — er — sub-humans to work for our cause.'

As usual Himmler did not notice the irony. 'All right, Major, I can see what you are getting at,' he said severely. 'But just remember one point — we are not here to liberate the Russians, but to colonise them. Now get on with it.'

The first hurdle cleared, Major von Kranz got down to explaining his plan. He got to his feet and crossed to the big map of the Russian front which covered one wall of the big office. 'Here in the south, Reichsführer, covering the approaches to the Caucasian oil fields which the Führer intends to capture this summer, two of our Army groups are preparing to launch Case Blue. One will strike from the Kursk-Kharkov area, the other from Taganrog west of Stalingrad. Once the jaws of their pincers meet and they have swallowed up the bulk of the enemy forces in the Don Basin, they will drive for the Caucasus and the oil fields —'

'Yes, I know all that,' Himmler interrupted irritably. 'I am kept well informed of what happens at the Führer HQ, Major von Kranz.'

'Sir! Well, when those jaws meet, Colonel von Manstein's Eleventh Army will find itself in the territory of the most rebellious and aggressive of all the anti-Soviet groups within that country — the territory of the Don Cossacks.' He paused momentarily and let the name sink in.

'The Cossacks,' Himmler echoed the name thoughtfully.

Outside, a group of ragged, bent prison inmates were dragging a cart piled with their own dead through the driving snow, urged on by Gestapo men armed with whips. 'Yes, the Cossacks,' Himmler repeated, 'a very warlike people. Ethnically much superior to the rest of that Slav pack, according to my researchers at the SS Race Office.'

'Yessir,' von Kranz seized the advantage, 'a warlike people which has been in constant opposition to the Soviet Regime ever since the days of the Revolution, first in the White Armies and then after they were defeated, in little armies which they formed themselves. Now sir, here,' he tapped the region of the Caucasus mountains, 'there is reported to be some four thousand of them, all proven rebels against the Bolsheviks. Indeed they are now little better than outlaws. They have nothing to lose and everything to gain by joining our side and,' he hurried on before Himmler could protest, 'helping us to open the door for Colonel-General von Manstein.'

'What do you mean, Major — open the door?' Himmler cut in, his eyes gleaming with sudden animation behind his steel-rimmed glasses.

'The door from the Crimea into the Caucasus.' He turned to the map again. 'You see the Parpach Isthmus blocks the passage of von Manstein's troops from the Crimea to the Kerch Isthmus, which is the logical springboard for any operation into the Caucasus. At present it is very heavily defended — our troops have been beaten off there twice already. But, sir, if the Russian troops were attacked from the rear in the same moment that our own soldiers attacked, the story might be very different.'

Himmler sucked his teeth thoughtfully as he pondered the crazy scheme, liking its boldness, yet wondering a little fearfully what the Führer's reaction might be if he discovered that the Reichsführer SS, the guardian of National Socialist purity, had used Russian soldiers for an operation.

In Himmler's bizarre dream world, the romantic vision of some sort of a medieval farm community in the east, peopled by blond giants, who ruled with an iron hand over their biologically inferior, bullet-headed dark Slav peasants, had become an almost sacred mission. In his dreams, he saw himself as one of those blond, blue-eyed giants, eternally young, capable of siring dozens of similarly fair-haired, blue-eyed children, who would turn the German nation into a folk of warrior peasants — the everlasting fountain of youth, replenishing the lifeblood of Germany', as he never tired of telling the Führer. Yet the Reichsführer knew, too, that as the situation stood at present, despite almost superhuman efforts, the Wehrmacht seemed incapable of forcing the decisive victory on the Russians; there were simply too many of the Slavs. As the young red-faced Major standing at the map had truly said, perhaps at this stage of the war one should compromise one's Aryan principles to beat the Russian; the reckoning could come thereafter.

He pursed his thin lips carefully. 'But Major, what you propose is a considerable military operation. We would have to find weapons and supplies to support your Cossacks in their trek across country, perhaps even air cover and I don't know what Fat Hermann would have to say about using his beloved Luftwaffe to support a bunch of Russian cowboys.' He smiled thinly and nodded at an impassive Teufel. 'My informants tell me that your Cossack general Kulakov is a legless cripple. No use for an operation of this type.' He pointed a thin finger almost accusingly at the Major. 'You would need to find a skilled military man with recent experience to undertake such a delicate task and I am sure you would not find him among a bunch of half-wild savages living little better than outlaws in those mountains down there.'

'I agree completely, Reichsführer,' von Kranz said eagerly. 'Definitely not among those Cossack outlaws, as you are pleased to call them.'

'Where then, man?' Himmler asked impatiently, while the Obersturmbannführer stared expectantly at the blond Major. 'Here, Reichsführer,' von Kranz announced triumphantly, rapping his knuckles against the map, 'In the Kazan Concentration Camp.'

CHAPTER 3

'The man that we on Field Marshal von Kluge's staff have in mind, Reichsführer,' von Kranz broke the surprised silence which had greeted his announcement, 'is Hetman Alexei of the Don Cossacks.'

'The Cossack leader,' Teufel explained hastily, not taking his dark eyes off von Kranz.

'Yes, that's right. Son of a Hetman himself, he joined the Imperial Army's Cossacks at the age of sixteen in 1916. Ever since then he has been constantly in action somewhere or other. As an ensign he won his first Cross of St George with the Nerchinsk Regiment in 1917. A year later, for some reason we don't understand he went over to the Bolsheviks and joined the Red Cossacks. At the age of eighteen he was a Hero of the Soviet Union and in charge of his own battalion. Two years later he was leading a Cossack Regiment against the Poles until Pilsudski stopped the Red Army outside Warsaw. He won his second Hero of the Soviet Union for his actions during the retreat to the Ukraine. His regiment was massacred but he managed to hold up a whole Polish cavalry division for a day. Thereafter they sent him to the Frunze Academy in Moscow for senior officer training where we lose him for a while until he turns up again in Manchuria in the fighting against those honorary Aryan allies of ours, the Japanese. That was in 1931. Then —'

Himmler held up his hand to stop the rapid flow of words. 'My dear Major, may I ask one question?'

'Yessir.'

'How is it,' Himmler smirked, 'that this paragon of Soviet military virtue is now in a concentration camp, eh?'

Von Kranz took a deep breath. 'That, too, is a long story, Reichsführer.'

'Well, make it short. Your time is running out, Major.'

'Well, sir, in thirty-six, the Russian Commander in Chief Vorosshilov, alarmed by our own re-armament, ordered the formation of five Cossack divisions, which were allowed to use the names of the old Cossack hordes — the Terek, the Kuban, etc. Hetman Alexei was given the rank of general and the charge of the new Don Cossack Cavalry Division. In order to avoid any internal trouble, the new Division was sent out to the Far East to train and it was there that Hetman Alexei came under the influence of Marshal Tukhachevskij.' He paused. 'You follow me, Reichsführer?'

Himmler's pale face broke into a wintry smile. He did indeed. Back in 1936, his most feared assistant SS General Reinhard Heydrich had planted evidence on the Russian Secret Service that the Russian Marshal, the most powerful figure in the Red Army and a former aristocrat to boot, was planning a *coup d'état* against Stalin himself. According to Heydrich's cunning plant, the Marshal, who was generally regarded as the 'saviour of the Red Revolution' within the Soviet Union, had wanted the assistance of the Wehrmacht to carry out his plan to get rid of Stalin, the Soviet dictator. As a result he had been arrested and sentenced to death. Thereafter a wholesale purge of the Red Army had followed. An orgy of liquidations had been the result so that by the end of 1938, the Russian Officer Corps had been reduced by fifty per cent and its higher ranks almost completely wiped out. It had been one of Heydrich's most successful international coups in his fight against world Communism.

'And this man of yours — Hetman Alexei — was one of those who were arrested, Major?'

'Yes Reichsführer. Although he was actively engaged on operations with his new division against the Japanese on the Manchurian border, he was paraded in front of his men, had his decorations stripped from him and was publicly beaten by the NKVD officers who had come from Moscow to arrest him. It must have been a tremendous humiliation for him, but he was lucky enough to escape with his life. Fortunately for him, his Division was on the verge of a mutiny at the manner of his arrest and so he was quickly whipped off to a concentration camp to serve an indeterminate sentence rather than being publicly tried.'

'I see, Major. You believe then that this Hetman Alexei of yours hates Stalin so bitterly that he would be prepared to take up arms against his native country in order to get his revenge?'

'Yes, Reichsführer. More, he is a well-trained officer of general's rank, who has already proved himself many times in battle. If anyone can rally those — er — outlaws in the Caucasus to our cause and lead them into the attack, it will be Hetman Alexei. Mind you, sir, they might demand a *Krug*.'

'A Cossack assembly,' Teufel explained swiftly.

Himmler looked thoughtful. 'If I agree to helping you on this somewhat improbable mission, who would be in charge of the team to rescue him from the concentration camp, Major?'

Major Peter von Kranz hesitated for a second. 'There would be no team, Reichsführer. Just one one man, who knows the country, the customs and the language intimately. Alone he stands a far better chance of getting Hetman Alexei out and back to the Cossacks in the mountains. Besides, I don't think it would be wise to let the Cossacks become too aware of the German presence behind Hetman.'

'Yes, that is indeed sensible. But who is this lone-handed hero of yours going to be, Major?'

'Me, sir.'

'Ach so, Sie, Herr Baron!'

Von Kranz flushed hotly. 'I know I can do it, Reichsführer. I know the area intimately. Before '39 I used to go hunting there from Riga with my father every winter. I know the people well. If you could arrange for the Zeppelin Squadron to drop me behind enemy lines, I am quite confident that I could pull it off. Whether he is prepared to go along with my scheme once I have penetrated the camp and contacted him — well, sir, that is the risk I have to take. But I shall contact him, come what may.'

Himmler held up his hand for peace. 'Good, good, my dear Baron! Now I can see how you won your tin — and lost your flipper too. Headstrong! I don't doubt your bravery. But one man alone. I don't like it, I don't like it at all.' He paused thoughtfully for a moment.

'You see, Major,' Himmler went on softly. 'I don't quite trust you gentlemen from the General Staff. I've heard the rumours that you intend to give the Russians some sort of independence when we have finally beaten the devils. What is it you are supposed to have planned — an independent Ukraine, perhaps even some form of White Russian state and so on.'

Von Kranz knew he was too close to success to start arguing with the Reichsführer SS now — the man was a fool, and that was that. He remembered von Tresckow's advice and repeated the very words the Colonel had said to him only two hours before across at the Bendlerstrasse: 'Sir, don't you think we should start worrying about Russia's future when we have conquered her?'

Himmler nodded. 'All right, Major, you have convinced me. You will receive my permission to borrow a Condor for your mission within the next twenty-four hours.'

'Thank you, sir. I am sure you won't regret it!'

'I *know* I won't,' Himmler said, smiling thinly. 'But please let me finish, Major. I have one condition to make.'

'Yessir.'

'That you will not go on this mission alone, Major. You will take one of my men with you.' He spun round on Teufel. 'Obersturmbannführer, I want you to accompany the Major on this operation.'

Teufel did not hesitate. 'Zu Befehl, Reichsführer.'

'Thank you, Teufel. I knew I could rely on you. Now the schnapps.'

The dark-eyed SS man turned and opened the cupboard on the wall. He took out the dark yellow bottle of Bavarian herbal liqueur which was all that the Reichsführer's sensitive stomach could tolerate. He filled three very small glasses (the Reichsführer was a very parsimonious man) with the nauseating stuff and handed them around. Himmler raised his glass to the third button of his black tunic as military etiquette demanded and with his elbow set at a ninety degree angle, he rapped: 'To the success of Operation Cossack! *Zum Wohle, meine Herren!*'

'To the success of Operation Cossack!' the young men answered as one, then drained their glasses and flung them on the floor.

KAZAN CONCENTRATION CAMP, MARCH 1942

CHAPTER 1

The big Cossack General lay on his bunk in the corner of the hut, listening to the mournful drip-drip of the spring rain, and considered the Fritzes' proposition.

At first it had shocked him. The two agents wanted him to betray his Fatherland: the country which had nurtured him and had made the son of a land-owning reactionary a General in the people's army; had laden him with honours and decorations. Hadn't he been the youngest full general in the Red Army after all?

But the handsome, one-armed Fritz had been prepared for his doubts. 'Look at that poster, General,' he had urged, pointing to the peeling black and red placard on one wall of the House of Culture — '*Dig Coal for the Fatherland*'. 'Can you see how the guards have erased the word "Fatherland". And why? Because all of you here are regarded as such monsters by Moscow that you must not be even allowed to see such a word as Fatherland. Don't you see, General, for you there is no Russian Fatherland! There is only the Fatherland of your own people and that is what we want you to fight for — not for Germany!'

Alexei ran a worried hand through his gleaming black hair. 'Fatherland,' he muttered to himself. 'What Fatherland?' History has its ghosts, and his people — the Don Cossacks — were historical ghosts, he told himself bitterly. Once the Cossacks had been Russia's pathfinders, its warrior explorers, who had opened Siberia up for the Czar, defeated Islam in the south and thrown back the Turks. For centuries the hard-riding Cossacks had fought and died everywhere for Russia, as if their lives had been as expendable as those of their horses which were shot from under them time and time again.

And what had been their reward? Oblivion. The map no longer showed their homeland and the Don Cossack people had been scattered over the face of the earth like the Jews in ancient times. In Hong Kong Cossack generals drove taxis for lousy Chinese businessmen. In Paris they had washed dishes for fat-bellied bourgeois in third-rate hotels and in London before the war they had sung sad songs for bored English milords.

He contained his anger at the injustice to his people, as he had done so many times before in the past. Hadn't he always told himself that the Russian workers were paying the Cossacks back for their crimes — for their cruelty and brutality in putting down strikes and anti-Czarist political meetings? One day it would all be forgotten and the Cossacks, the sons and daughters of those old, dead reactionaries with their knouts and sabres, would be accepted into the new Soviet society?

And yet hadn't he, a soldier who had been completely devoted to the Soviet cause (so much so that his father had disowned him as a traitor to the Don Cossack people), been publicly humiliated in front of his own soldiers — sixteen thousand of them? On that burning hot day his life had been destroyed. After twenty years of loyal service to Russia, he had been treated worse than a common criminal, thrown into prison without trial, not even allowed to see his wife and child. He thought of Vera, so blonde and beautiful. Dead now, these two years — suicide, according to the rumours which had filtered into him from outside — while her son had vanished, probably put in some NKVD orphanage under an assumed name so that one day he could become a 'loyal' Soviet citizen.

Alexei raised his head slightly and stared down at his heavy, muscular, naked arms, criss-crossed with sabre scars from the battles of the Civil War. He had shed his blood for the wrong side; he realised that now. He should have joined his father and the Whites. But that was history. What of the present? What was he going to do?

He let his head sink back on the wooden pillow, his harshly handsome face thoughtful. Outside the drip-drip of the rain began to die away. To the east, the sun was beginning to flood the dark sky with its warming rays.

'Well?' the tall blond German with one arm hissed urgently, 'what have you decided General?'

Beside him the dark-eyed SS man tensed against the wall of the latrine, his hand dug deep in the pocket of his ragged jacket, as if he were holding on tightly to some weapon concealed there. The Fritz was scared, Alexei could see that, very scared.

Alexei forced a smile, feeling the warming rays of the sun on his back. 'Let me ask you a question first, Major? Why are you so interested in the welfare of the Cossack horde, or whatever you want to call that bunch of outlaws you told me about?'

Despite his tenseness, the German smiled too and Alexei liked him for it. 'Naturally, General, the German Wehrmacht is not solely concerned with the welfare of your Cossacks. Generals, if you'll forgive me, *General*, are not very charitable people on the whole!'

'I take your point — carry on.'

'Well, I can't give you full details at this moment, General. But in return for your freedom and our support, my chiefs expect you to convince those Cossacks down there to follow you on a small operation we have planned.'

'*Convince*,' Alexei echoed. 'Not so easy, Major. Remember I am a traitor to the Cossack cause as they see it. After all I did fight against them in the Civil War and I was a senior officer in the Red Army. But go on, first things first. What is this operation you have planned?'

Alexei noted the warning look the SS officer flashed to his companion, but the German Major did not hesitate. 'General, you must understand that I can't give you full details at the moment for obvious reasons. But in essence, we expect you to carry out a small operation to the rear of the Red Army front at its southern base. Then you will pass over into our lines.'

Alexei laughed drily. 'So that's it! You Fritzes are going to launch your spring offensive in the south this year. Where's it going to be — the Rostov-Kursk area? And what are you after — Stalingrad or will your troops turn south and go after the Caucasian oil?' He looked at the two Germans knowingly.

The Fritzes flushed. Obviously his prediction had been too accurate. For a moment no one spoke and he allowed himself to enjoy the sun. Outside the steppe was beginning to steam now with the sudden heat and Alexei wondered what it must be like to be astride a fine horse once more, galloping over the spring new grass that had been hidden beneath the winter snow. Suddenly he was overcome with the heady, almost painful desire to be free again. 'All right,' he broke the silence suddenly, 'what plans have you for getting me out of this place, Major, eh?'

Major von Kranz, who had begun to realise that he must not underestimate Hetman Alexei, answered swiftly. 'Well, General, we thought the same way as we got into this camp. We've done it twice now without anyone taking the slightest bit of notice of us. Once we have you in the outer camp, we march out the next morning with the first working party, and vanish.'

Alexei shook his head. 'Quite impossible. Look at me, Major.' He drew himself up to his full height, his chest threatening to burst through the immaculate, if worn cloth of his *Cherkesska*. 'I stick out like a sore thumb here. Every guard knows me — after all it isn't every day that some little Siberian private soldier has the chance of ordering around a full general, is it. No, I wouldn't even get close to the gate. I am too recognisable. And it would give the *Natschalnik* — that filthy NKVD torturer — the greatest pleasure to report to Moscow that I had been shot while attempting to escape. After he had enjoyed the sadistic pleasure of stripping the flesh off my bones with that damn cruel knout of his.'

'But what other way is there?'

But before Alexei had time to answer, the morning air was full of the sound of excited female voices and the splashing of hurrying feet through the steaming puddles.

Hastily Alexei grabbed the Major's arm and pulled him behind the wall. 'Quick,' he hissed to the SS man, 'here!'

A moment later a confused procession of women came into sight, filling the muddy square off the House of Culture, gesticulating, laughing and shouting, their whole attention concentrated on the beautiful young woman in their midst, who strode through the mud like a royal princess.

'Who in the heaven's name is that?' Viktor asked in awe.

'The great whore herself,' Alexei hissed. 'The Zariza!'

Somehow Major von Kranz had expected her to be an old, gross, blowsy woman, something like the great eighteenth century libertine Empress Catherine the Great with whom the old *Starosta* had compared her. But the Zariza was a slim, petite woman, dwarfed by the half-naked bulk of the gypsy procuress, who had dragged away the prisoner the first night. She was young too, with her pale blonde hair freshly curled, stuck tight to the sides of her well-formed head in the style of the twenties. Suddenly she turned and stared at the House of Culture. Peter von Kranz caught a glimpse of a mocking, sensual mouth, smouldering bedroom eyes and the livid weal of a knife scar which ran down the left side of her face. Then Alexei's big hand descended upon his shoulder and forced him to the ground.

'Get down both of you,' he ordered urgently and dropped beside them. 'That one is like a child — a perverted pretty child,' he explained. 'She wants anything handsome she sees in trousers and that great mare of a maid with her ensures she gets what she wants...'

Finally the raucous cries and hysterical cursing of the *Blatnajas* died away. Cautiously the Cossack General raised himself and indicated they should do the same.

'So that was the Zariza?' Viktor remarked, dusting the dirt off his knees.

'Yes, that is the mare who runs this camp,' Alexei said thoughtfully. 'And it is through the hole she provides — you'll excuse the crudity? — that we shall escape.'

'But what do you mean?' the SS man objected. 'Through the hole she provides?' His dark face was as cold and as suspicious as ever.

'The Zariza, Fritz,' Alexei lectured him, 'is the real power in this camp. If she wishes, she can provide us with everything we need. An escape route, food, transport, perhaps even weapons.'

'But why should she?' Viktor persisted.

In answer Alexei made the obscene Russian gesture of thrusting the tip of his thumb between his two forefingers. 'Because of that! Someone must service that mare — and if she's satisfied, she might help. I hate the whore and she knows that. Twice that procuress has made approaches to me, but I made it quite clear to the cow that I'd have the great udders off her, if she tried anything. So we agreed to go our separate ways. But still the Zariza is interested — that much I know.'

'You mean?'

'Of course,' the grin spread across Alexei's face. 'I'll bed the mare and by God, I'll satisfy her too.'

CHAPTER 2

The Zariza lay on the big bed, covered in a white silk sheet, clad in nothing but a pair of black sheer panties as the big gypsy pushed open the door and led the General inside, a knife held protectively in her big fist. 'The prick,' she announced in her gruff voice.

The Zariza looked up, a half-smile on her mocking lips. 'So you have finally come to visit me, my dear General,' she said. 'I have waited a long time.'

Alexei did not reply at once. Instead he looked around the room, lit a dusky red from the stove and a solitary candle burning underneath a red glass mantle. The place was decorated in a style current at the turn of the century. Heavy, red velvet tasselled curtains hung from the windows. Brass ornaments were everywhere. The unlit table lamps were covered with long fringed silken shades and on the floor there were at least three Bukhara rugs. Then his eye fell on the bottle of *Gorilka* vodka on the table, which was covered in green felt and bound with aggressive brass studs. 'A little ray of sunshine in the stomach, mare!' he ordered the maid in his deep bass. The woman looked at him angrily, her jaw clenched threateningly, and then at the Zariza.

'Give him it,' she ordered, 'and me one too.'

Her face flushed, the maid walked across to the table and poured two water glasses full of the Ukrainian vodka.

The General raised his glass. 'Zariza — love and money!'

The Zariza raised her glass. 'Love and money,' she repeated.

Slowly and deliberately, the General stalked across the room in his highly polished, if down-at-heel riding boots, took the

Zariza's pale hand in his and raised it courteously to his lips. 'I have come to spend the night with you, Zariza — please send your creature away.'

'*Creature,*' the maid exploded. 'Who do —'

The Zariza silenced her with an imperious wave of her hand.

'Enough,' she cried. 'You may go — *now!*' For an instant, her sultry eyes flashed a warning: a warning that the other woman could read and understand.

She backed out without another word.

'She was once my lover,' the Zariza said softly. 'I got this,' she fingered the livid weal, 'in a fight for her. But please, General, take a seat. And remove your *Cherkesska.* The night is young and we have a lot of drinking —'

'And loving to do,' the General finished as he removed his Cossack coat in a swift movement.

As he took the rest of his clothes off she ran her glowing eyes over the hairy chest, powerful, almost brutal arms, scarred here and there by old sabre cuts from the battles of the Civil War. The Zariza's nose twitched in delight as she drank in his heavy smell. 'You stink of man!' she hissed. 'Sweat and earth and man!'

She quivered with desire and closed her eyes.

Above her blonde tousled head, Alexei heard the sighing shudder of pleasure, and knew that he was in full control. The vodka had dampened his initial passion at seeing a beautiful naked woman after so many months without love. Now he knew he could go on all night. He knew too that not only his escape but his life depended upon his ability to satisfy the Zariza in a way she had never been satisfied before.

He played with her body the whole night. Until finally he allowed the wild wave of orgasm to sweep over him in a burst of exquisite glory. Then he stopped and let himself slip into a sweat-lathered exhausted sleep.

It was nearly dawn. Outside they could hear the first slow sounds of the camp coming to life in preparation for another cruel day; the rattle of the cooks' tins, the thick consumptive cough of some pain-racked prison orderly, the soft howls of the guard dogs, grateful that the night was over, hungry for their morning rations.

She lay on the rumpled, sweat-soaked bed, still naked, dark circles under her eyes, her blonde hair tousled and disordered, sipping the pink Crimean champagne and watching him shrewdly, as he roused himself from his exhausted sleep. She nodded at the champagne.

He shook his tousled head. 'No,' he said thickly through his scummed lips, 'I want fire.' Naked as he was, he padded across the room to the vodka bottle. He filled half a water glass and downed it in one. 'Good,' he said, and wiped the liquid from his lips.

Alexei sat down opposite the Zariza, knowing that the time had come for him to make his request. The great whore looked relaxed, satiated, happy with him, though he did not quite like the shrewd look in her eyes. Still he would have to ask her before the others came; then he would make love to her again — tremendously — and set the seal on their arrangement.

Slowly he reached out and ran his calloused, cavalryman's palm across the warm naked skin of her breasts. She shuddered a little with new and remembered pleasure and her nipples immediately grew erect. A little painfully she shifted her position to kiss his hand and he could see the bloodstains on the bed from the beating he had given her. But her eyes still did not lose their shrewd look.

'I need your help, Zariza,' he said carefully.

'So.' She considered for a moment, still holding his hand in hers. 'Is that why you came here?'

'In a way.'

'What way?' In spite of the first new stirrings of sexual pleasure that were beginning to flush her face, the question was precise and posed with the autocratic authority of a woman who had once been the mistress of the second most powerful man in the Soviet state.

'Zariza, my little dove, I must leave the camp,' he said gruffly.

Slowly she let go of his hand and looked at him, as if she were seeing him for the first time. 'Leave? You mean escape?'

He nodded.

'But where would you go?'

'To my own people, the Cossacks. Back to the Quiet Don.'

'But what will you do there?' she objected. 'You know as well as I do that Lavrenti Pavlovich's people will find you in the end.'

'Zariza, I must take a chance on that. I shall go back to my native stanitsa. There the Cossacks will hide me in the forests when the NKVD come looking for me. If I'm lucky, they won't find me. If I'm unlucky, then —' he drew his big forefinger across his neck to indicate what would happen to him. 'But even that would be better than this hell, Zariza. I am used to horses, the wide steppe, space. Here I am like a dog in a tight kennel. I must get out.'

She indicated the vodka bottle. 'Another little ray of sunshine for your stomach,' she suggested, 'while I think a moment, General.'

Obediently he padded across to the bottle of *Gorilka*, his back to her. Thus he did not see the new look in her dark eyes:

a mixture of pain from her lacerated back, where he had flogged her, and sly cunning.

He downed the vodka and turned round to face her again, his hairy body again displaying its aggressive naked maleness. 'Well, my little dove, will you help me?'

Her pink tongue slid between her dry lips and licked them in anticipation. Almost automatically her slim white legs opened once again.

'Well, Zariza?'

She reached out her arms to him, her face strained with sexual desire. 'Yes, I shall help you, General. Come!'

The old pain and her plan of revenge left for a while. A new pleasurable one took possession of her, making her gasp and moan and thrash and claw the length of the General's broad muscular back, as she pleaded with him never to stop.

CHAPTER 3

'Well?' Peter asked, as they crouched in the latrine of the central camp, the spring rain still beating a noisy tattoo on its tin roof.

Hetman Alexei nodded. 'Yes, it worked. The bitch tore my back to ribbons with her nails, but I suppose it was worth it.' He grinned suddenly. 'It was good to have a woman again, I can tell you.'

'That I can believe,' Peter agreed, smiling at the Cossack General. 'Even on the food in this place, I'm beginning to feel the need myself.'

'Ach,' Viktor cried angrily, 'can't the two of you drop the subject of women and get on with it? Will she or won't she help us?'

Alexei looked at him in mild contempt, as if he were little better than the black bugs scuttling across the muddy floor of the latrine. 'Of course, she will help us. Apparently I satisfied the mare... According to her, the *Blatnajas* have a perfect escape route.'

'Where General?'

'Under the House of Culture. We were standing above it the other day. Those criminals of hers know everything there is to know about the camp naturally. They have to if they want to survive. Now according to the Zariza, when the camp was built the House of Culture was the *Natschalnik's* headquarters. Naturally such an important personage as that Siberian torturer had to have a proper latrine for himself and his staff. No thunderboxes such as these for them to rest their delicate arses on. No, the real thing with chains and running water for them

71

— why most of the Siberian bastards were wiping their arses with their hands only a couple of years back!'

Peter grinned at the Cossack, but Viktor's dark face remained as sour and sombre as ever.

'So, the *Natschalnik* had a proper sewage system built which leads out of the camp and on to that lake at the edge of the forest. You know it?'

They nodded.

'Now apparently the Zariza's people have been using it for their own illegal activities in and out of camp for some time, and this morning she promised me she would reveal where it is located to me. In addition, she'll provide us with food for seven days.' He hesitated momentarily. 'But no weapons, although I'm damn sure they've got plenty of them hidden about the camp somewhere or other.'

Peter looked keenly at the Cossack's suddenly worried face. 'Why did you say it like that, General?' he asked.

'Because I don't trust the bitch.'

'What?' Viktor asked in alarm.

'It was too easy,' Alexei said thoughtfully. Why should a woman like that whose mind is between her legs want to relinquish — er — my services. If she liked me so much, why let me go? No, no, Major, that whore has got something up her sleeve, believe me.'

Zariza had made up her mind to betray the General to the camp authorities by the time her maid had returned at midday to give her her daily bath.

The maid prepared the towels and the perfumes to be used, then ordered the women to fill the tin bath, while the Zariza lay silently on the bed. Finally the maid was satisfied and clapped her hands for the shabby servants to depart. T

The Zariza was strangely lethargic. The maid gasped when she saw what was revealed under her mistresses undergarments. 'Who ... who did that to you?' she gasped. 'The Cossack,' the Zariza answered and winced with pain.

'Oh, my poor mistress,' the maid cried. 'How could that swine do a thing like that to you?'

'He beat me — and then he did something else, something very cruel that no other man — not even Lavrenti Pavlovich himself — would have dared do to the Zariza if he valued his life,' she whispered, her voice hoarse as if in pain, her dark eyes suddenly filled with tears.

The maid was overcome by a sudden rage at the sight of the tears in her mistress's eyes. 'That Cossack prick — I'll rip it off him with my own bare hands — slowly! I'll tear it in two! I'll feed it to him — bit by bit, as he lies there dying on the floor ... I'll...'

The Zariza raised her hand for the crimson-faced maid to be quiet. 'You say you would rip the Cossack apart.' She shook her blonde head. 'That would be too obvious. We won't do it.' The Zariza's eyes smouldered with both revenge and pleasure. 'I want to see him punished — slowly — in the same way that he punished me last night — with the knout.'

'The *Natschalnik*?'

The Zariza nodded.

'What are your orders?'

'You will show them the passage and ensure that the *Natschalnik* knows that he can expect an escaper near the lake. He does not need to know how our man has got there.' She laughed carelessly. 'Not that that will bother him, as long as he can indulge in one of his sadistic orgies.'

'And in return for the information?' the maid asked.

'In return, the Zariza would like to observe the punishment he deals out to the prisoner. You understand, Katya?' the Zariza shuddered with delight at the thought of the whipping soon to come.

The camp was silent save for the soft howl of the wind and the ever present pad-pad of the dogs in the outer wire. Softly for such a huge woman, the lesbian appeared at the door to the House of Culture, the sack of provisions in her hand.

Hastily she thrust the bag into the waiting General's hand and crooked her finger at him to indicate that he should follow her. He needed no urging. He sped after her noiselessly, his boots covered by a pair of old woollen socks. She led him down the gloomy, blacked out corridor, past the library, which contained nothing but Lenin's works, *Das Kapital* and a tattered copy of the *Eighteenth Brumaire* in German, and into the storage area.

She stopped and looked cautiously up the dirty corridor. No-one in sight. She flung back her cloak to reveal she was stripped to the waist as usual, with one exception — a small key hung round her bull neck, attached to the end of a frayed black shoelace. Hastily she took it off and fitted it into the door of the nearest cubby-hole. The lock snapped back immediately, as if it had been well-oiled recently. 'In there,' she said, breaking her silence for the first time.

He followed her inside the musty smelling, gloomy little hole. With the heel of her man's boot, she kicked the door closed behind her and bent down, her naked breasts dangling to her knees. She grunted.

A door opened up in the middle of the floor, and the stench hit the General in the face with almost physical force. He swallowed hard. 'Is this it?' he asked thickly, trying not to breathe in the thick, cloying odour of ancient human waste.

The lesbian laughed at the look on his tense face. 'The honest stink of human shit. Comrade General. You'll get used to it after a while.'

'Yes,' he answered, 'your presence is rapidly accustoming me to it.' Her dark gypsy face flushed angrily. 'Off with you prick, before I speed you on your way with the toe of my boot!'

He made an obscene gesture with his finger and poising himself above the hole, let go. In an instant he disappeared into the stinking darkness.

For a moment the lesbian looked at the hole, then she laughed. It was not a pleasant sound. She kicked the cover swiftly back into place and closing the door behind her, bustled down the dark corridor to find the Camp Commandant. In her haste she did not see the two ragged prisoners crouching expectantly in the shadows.

The journey down the sewer had been a nightmare. Sometimes they had been forced to wade through the stinking filth up to their knees. At other places the lowness of the lime encrusted, dripping roof had forced them to crawl on their hands and knees, following the flickering light of the General's hissing white carbide lamp. But the General had brooked no hesitation.

Once Viktor had halted with a stifled gasp of fear. A gigantic, terrifying shadow blocked the way through the hideously bubbling mess. 'What's that?' he had cried fearfully.

The General had chuckled softly. 'Now, don't you be adding any more to this mess, Fritz,' he had soothed him. 'It's nothing but a rat!' In the same instant he had kicked his dripping foot against the side of the lime encrusted wall. There had been the soft patter of clawed feet and the monster had disappeared. They had pushed on.

Now, however, the sewer was beginning to grow a little lighter, and Peter von Kranz imagined that the fetid air seemed to be growing a little cooler, as if the wind were blowing it in across the surface of the lake. Alexei held up his hand for them to halt and blew out the carbide lamp. 'I don't think we're far off now,' he said softly. 'The time has come for me to go on alone.'

Peter bit his bottom lip anxiously. 'Do you think we should do it as you suggested, General?'

Alexei drew himself up, the best he could in the narrow confines of the sewer, every inch a general. 'Of course, have I not made my plan? I shall allow myself to be captured by that Siberian turd. He does not know of your presence. Thus he will be caught off guard. His mind will be full of the nasty little tricks he will want to play on my body. It should be easy for you.'

'But what if there are a lot of them?' Viktor objected, his face stained with the mire. 'What then?'

The General shook his head. 'Ah, Fritz, you are always so optimistic! Don't worry. We Cossacks say that if a hunchbacked dwarf catches a giant with his trousers down, all he has to do to beat him is to reach up and pull twice.' He laughed softly, an uncanny sound in that strange stinking place. 'We shall catch the *Natschalnik* off guard, believe me. All you need to do is to reach up and pull twice. Now let's stop the talking and get on with it eh?' He tugged at his *Cherkesska* and turned to go. 'Once they've got me — come quick,' he said over his shoulder.

'Don't worry, we'll come,' Peter von Kranz replied. 'And General — good luck.'

'Cossacks don't need luck, Baron,' the General answered, chuckling throatily, 'they make it with their own cunning.' And with that, he was gone, slithering through the mire towards the opening with surprising speed for such a big man.

The camp was well blacked out. The only light he could see as he emerged from the sewer and crouched there, breathing in the cold fresh air gratefully, was the twin circles of icy white cast on the ground by the lamps over the main gate. Everything was quiet. There was no sound save for the gentle rustle of the wind. It seemed as if the whole world were asleep. For one brief instant he wondered whether he had misjudged the Zariza; perhaps she didn't intend to betray him after all.

Suddenly he stiffened. A dark shape had moved in the naked bushes to the left. He turned his head to one side and with the old Cossack trick brought his head up at an angle so that he could focus better. Yes, there was no doubt about it. There was someone standing there. And behind him someone else. The *Natschalnik* was waiting for him.

He straightened up. 'All right, my little Chinese turd,' he told himself, 'let me see how you scream this time.' Taking a deep breath, he began to walk towards the bushes, stumbling a little over the uneven ground in the thick darkness.

'*Stoi?*' an excited high-pitched voice cut the darkness. An instant later a torch flashed on. He flung his arm up in front of his face, blinded by the sharp white light.

'It's him, *Natschalnik*!' someone cried excitedly.

There was a heavy rush of feet. His arm still held in front of his face to cut out the blinding light, the General counted them. Four of them, including the *Natschalnik* mounted as ever on his great white stallion. A whip curled around the General's shoulders with excruciating pain. 'So,' the *Natschalnik's* thin insidious voice rapped, 'our dear Cossack has suddenly developed home sickness for his Quiet Don, eh?' Again the whip curled viciously across the prisoner's shoulders. 'I think we'll have to cure him of that particular affliction. All right, soldiers, bind him!'

Noiselessly, on cats' feet, Viktor and Peter sneaked up on the four figures grouped round the General. They were talking excitedly among themselves. 'Viktor,' Peter whispered in the other man's ear. 'Leave the two tying up the General. Take the one with the rifle. I'll take the one on the horse.'

'Good.'

They were only fifteen metres away now. The Russians had still not heard them. Viktor pulled out his wire loop. Next to him, Peter slid the safety off the little battery-powered pistol. He must bring the horseman down before he had a chance to gallop away and raise the alarm. As the General had planned it, everything had to be done swiftly and with as little noise as possible.

'*Now!*' he hissed urgently.

They darted forward. Almost before the NKVD men were aware they were being attacked, Viktor had his noose around the neck of the man with a rifle, had forced him on his knees, and with his boot planted in the small of the Russian's back, was garrotting the life out of him with exquisite cruelty.

Peter fired. There was a soft hiss and the little gun trembled in his hand. The *Natschalnik* slid gently from his big horse and slumped to the ground.

'*Pyos!*' one of the men tying up the General cursed in terror. He swung round. Peter caught a glimpse of a contorted, frightened face. In that same moment, the General aimed a mighty kick at the guard. It caught him between the legs. The vomit shot out of his mouth and he lay on the wet earth, writhing frantically from side to side in agony.

Peter fired again. The other guard clapped his hand to his shoulder with a yelp of pain. He spun round, his rifle tumbling to the ground, to be met by the General's clubbed, tied fists. He fell to the ground without another sound, and lay still.

Swiftly Viktor sprang up from the man he had strangled to death and began fumbling with the General's bonds. The General grinned at him hugely. 'Didn't I tell you, Fritz, that my plan would work? I had thought of everything in advance — that's why I outwitted that Siberian turd.' He aimed a vicious kick on the *Natschalnik's* dead body sprawled dead under the hooves of his trembling white horse. 'You can —'

He broke off suddenly. Somewhere in the darkness of the bushes, something had moved. The three escapers froze, their heads on one side, straining to identify the sound. Peter felt the palm of his hand, which held the little pistol, suddenly wet with sweat. For a moment nothing happened. Then, there it was again. And this time there was no mistaking it. It was the soft pad-pad of a dog's paws. General Alexei had overlooked one thing.

The *Natschalnik* had brought one of the vicious, half-wild Alsatians with him.

Peter's heart skipped a beat wildly. One burst of barking from the dog and the sentries in their stork-legged towers would be pumping lead in their direction a second later.

'Freeze — the two of you!' Alexei hissed urgently.

They did as they were ordered, but Peter could not banish the mental picture he had of the Alsatians with their open dripping jaws and long yellow vicious teeth.

Suddenly the dog smelled them. It veered to the right. Desperately Peter fumbled for his tiny pistol. He had one bullet left. He would have to kill the half-wild animal with it, but kill it so that it had no chance to alarm the sentries. It came closer then stopped again, a stark black outline against the bleak horizon, raising its long snout and sniffing the air.

For a long moment, Peter thought that the long-haired brute, would go past them. But he was mistaken. As it started to lope forward again, it came straight for them. A second more, and it would bump into them as they crouched there, tense and breathless, among the dead NKVD men. Slowly he began to raise his pistol. The Alsatian spotted them. It stopped about three metres away and let out a low growl. It sank back slightly on its powerful haunches, its wet upper lip curled upwards, it's long yellow teeth bared hideously. Peter knew the signs from his father's hunting dogs before the war. It was preparing to spring.

He raised his pistol and took careful aim. At his side Viktor gasped, and in the same instant the dog launched itself into space in a great, open-fanged leap. Peter pressed the trigger but nothing happened.

The Alsatian's eighty pounds of hard, tense muscle struck him full in the chest. He collapsed under the weight, his nostrils full of the nauseating sickly sweat odour of dog, his face swamped in wriggling fur. Desperately he tried to get free, struggling wildly under the writhing mass. A paw swiped his face. Cruel claws ripped its length, splattering blood everywhere. The smell of the warm blood seemed to send the dog crazy. Twisting its head violently, it sought for Peter's throat with its jaws, its saliva dropping sickeningly on the agent's fear contorted face.

It was then that Alexei broke the spell of horror. He launched himself forward in a shallow dive. He jammed his arm between Peter's face and the dog. He yelled as the Alsatian sank its cruel claws into his arm, but the pain did not prevent him making his next move. With his other hand, he sought and found what was the great, half-wild dog's weak point. Like an iron vice, his fingers squeezed and held the animal's genitals. He pressed harder. The dog released the grip on his arm. The excruciating pain stopped. But he had no time to notice. 'Fritz,' he hissed, 'Grab it, for God's sake!'

Viktor flung himself on top of the dog. At the same moment, Alexei freed his grip on the dog's genitals. The Alsatian opened its jaws to howl, but Alexei's hands shot to its raised throat and stifled the howl at birth. The dog and the man rolled back and forth on the damp ground, while slowly and inevitably he squeezed the life out of it with his great iron hands. The Alsatian gave one last heave, its body as tense as a bow. Then the life went from it.

Alexei raised himself slowly and breathed out hard. 'The bastard is dead,' he sighed. 'I thought it was never going to die.' Contemptuously he turned the dead dog over with his boot. 'But then these German imports do not have the stamina of our native Russian dogs. If it had been a Borzoi,' he shrugged expressively, 'that would have been another story.'

Peter grinned and wiped the blood from his ripped face. 'Come on, General. We haven't time to go into that now.

We've got to put a lot of ground between us and the camp before the guards discover the *Natschalnik* is missing in the morning.'

Rather less than two hours later, they had dug the *Abwehr* Afu radio set up from the spot where they had buried it in the forest almost a week before and transmitted the agreed message. 'Operation Cossack, successful... Over and out... '

A few minutes afterwards they had disappeared into the forest. Their long journey to the Caucasus had begun.

THE DON VALLEY, MARCH 1942

CHAPTER 1

The abandoned shed in which the three of them had spent the night stank of rotten straw and the dried dung which the peasants used as fuel in winter. But despite their depressing surroundings this morning, the General was in high spirits as he rubbed some of the dry dung up and down between his hands, shredding it rapidly so that he could use it as tobacco in the Russian fashion. They had been free for two days now on the horses they had taken from the dead NKVD men, with the General leading them steadily south on the *Natschalnik's* fine white stallion. Twice they had almost bumped into Red Army cavalry patrols; twice the General had led them out of danger, warned in advance by a sixth sense.

Now the three of them were restive — after forty-eight hours of hard riding, and waiting for dusk when they planned to set out again. For they were close to the front and what peasants were left on the collective farms of the area would be forced home early by the curfew. After dark the only people they would meet would be Red Army troops.

But the night was still a long way off and now the three of them luxuriated in the first warming rays of the sun beginning to filter through the holes in the thatched roof. While the two Germans lazed, the General, elated to be free once more and puffing hard at his primitive cigarette to keep it alight, regaled them with the stories of his Cossack youth and their fighting lore.

'You must remember,' he lectured them, 'that the Cossack was a special type of warrior. Not really a people but a military order. One's father was a soldier, and his father, and his father before him. Why my grandfather served in the army for thirty years as did most of the fit men of that day. Fighting was a family tradition and the average fit man could not visualise any other kind of life.

'The Cossack needed no drill sergeant to teach him how to fight,' Alexei continued. 'His father taught him that. Perhaps you have seen our old Cossack villages with their broad streets and big squares — almost like parade grounds? Well in those streets and squares on Sundays and holidays, double rows of saplings used to be set up so that the fathers could teach their young sons how to gallop between the rows slashing at them with a sabre without cutting off the tops.'

'But don't heads roll, General, when Cossacks fight?' Peter asked.

Alexei shook his head. 'Only when the Cossack is a bad fighter. A skilled Cossack slashes his sabre down like this.' His hand cut through the air, as if he were back in the saddle, wielding the heavy curved Cossack sword of his youth. 'Deep into the side of his enemy's throat so that the head settles down but doesn't roll off the body. And that was only one of the strokes the old men used to teach their sons when I was a boy on the Don.'

'What were the others?' Peter encouraged him, while Viktor sat in silence, eyes closed, his face turned up to the sun's warming rays.

Alexei shrugged. 'It all depends upon the enemy you're fighting. If he's a little fellow, the Cossack will cleave his skull like this. If he is a big fellow, he will use the slash to the throat or across the spine from the shoulder to the hip. The trick is not to let your sabre be caught in the wound which would make you defenceless in a cavalry mêlée. Oh, there were lots of things that the Cossack father used to teach his sons when I was a boy. How to cross a stream without letting his mount stir up any water which might give him away. How to bend right down and lash his horse's hooves — not its neck or rump — when it begins to flag. How to pull his cap over his ears in the morning so that he cannot hear his mother's pleas when he gallops away to fight. Yes, in those days before the Revolution, our boys grew up having pride in their fathers and their warrior ancestors. Besides the Cossack always fought together with people from his own village. Each village formed its own company so that the Cossack didn't only fight for his Fatherland but for his own family and the village. That made him fearless, because he knew he could never go home again if he showed cowardice on the battlefield. In war he did not know the meaning of the word "no" — only that of "yes". Whatever obstacle he met, he knew he had to overcome it, cost what it may. Why, when I was a young man in the Nerchinsk Regiment, we always wore red waistcoats so that if we were wounded, the blood wouldn't show up and reveal to our enemies how weak we really were.' The big Cossack's dark, handsome face hardened suddenly and he rubbed his hand slowly over his unshaven chin. 'For five hundred years we Cossacks played a decisive part in every battle that has been fought on this bloody soil — and believe me, Major,' he added with sudden resolve, 'given half a chance, we'll do the same again.'

'I believe you, General. My chief Field Marshal von Kluge has the greatest confidence in the Cossack horde's fighting ability.'

Alexei looked at him searchingly, his dark eyes narrowed in the smoke of his evil-smelling cigarette. 'Is that why you are here, Major? Just because you have been ordered to by your Field Marshal?'

'In part, General, naturally. But you see, General, we Baltic Germans served the Czar for many centuries. We are of German blood, yet we are Russians too. My father, for example, loved Russia — he shed his blood for it in the other war, fighting against the same Wehrmacht in which I now serve. In his honour, I should like to see the red perversion destroyed and a new, free Russia established. You see, General, your Cossacks are the only part of the great plan. I, and those in Germany like me, want freedom for the whole of Mother Russia, but that new Russia must not be forced on the people by German arms alone. Those Russians who oppose Stalin and his gang must help us to bring about his downfall.'

General Alexei turned to Viktor, squatting on a heap of dried dung. 'And you?' his voice deep and commanding, 'why are you here?'

Slowly Viktor Teufel opened his eyes. At that moment his dark, wolfish face with its slanting Tartar eyes lived up to his name. 'Why am I here? Because I have been ordered to and because with your help we Germans will destroy the Communist perversion, wipe it and all those who are part of it from the face of this accursed Russia —'

'Viktor!' Peter cut in angrily. 'Will you stop this!'

The General held up a hand to silence the Major. 'Let him speak,' he said. 'After all he is risking his life just as we are. He has a right to speak his piece.'

'For centuries,' Viktor said, his gaze directed into space, as if he could not bear to look at the other two, 'we Volga Germans served Russia loyally. We worked hard, very hard, paid our taxes, and when the call came, we went to fight for the Czar and Russia. Later when the Bolsheviks came, we fought for them too. Think of Marshal Bluecher, for example — he was one of us. But how did you Russians repay us for our loyalty in the end? By robbery, beatings, the confiscation of our land, exile — and death!

'Always you Russians have envied us our industry, our wealth, our land, because you were lazy, easygoing, too much concerned with your drinking and skirt-chasing to get any real work done.' Alexei saw how the Fritz's eyes were filled with hatred.

'But in 1941 at the start of the German campaign in this damned land, you Russians finally transformed your envy into brutal slaughter, didn't you?'

'How do you mean, little brother?' the General asked gently. 'Remember I have been in the camp these last three years.'

Viktor's look of naked hate did not soften. 'When I went to Germany in the early thirties, my mother and my young sister stayed behind on the farm. Why should they move? In those days before the Führer rescued Germany, there were six million unemployed in the Reich. Admittedly our farm had been collectivised, but Moscow was far away and we Volga Germans always stuck together. So they stayed behind. After all Russia was their homeland — Germany was a foreign country. But what did Moscow do when the victorious German army started to show you what real soldiers were in '41?'

The two others said nothing.

'I'll tell you what those bastards in Moscow did! They used planes disguised as German aircraft to drop leaflets on the Volga populace, urging them to rise and support the advancing German troops. When a few hundred fools fell for the trick and did just that, the NKVD moved into the area in divisional strength. They slaughtered my people by the thousand, burning their homes, uprooting them from their farms, deporting whole communities to God knows where.' He looked at

Alexei, his dark Tartar eyes burning with hate. 'A whole people has been liquidated, General. It wasn't just my mother and sister, but a whole damned people. All gone now, disappeared from the face of the earth, never to be seen again, in my opinion. Now can you understand, why I want to see this damned, damned country trodden down into the dust?'

'But Viktor,' Peter tried to calm him, placing his one hand on the SS officer's shoulder.

Viktor shrugged it off angrily, rose to his feet and stamped outside.

For a moment or two, Alexei and Peter sat staring at each other in heavy silence. Then Alexei said slowly, 'Among my people, Major, we say "scratch a Russian and you'll find a Tartar. But scratch a Tartar and you'll find — a Tartar!"' With a jerk of his head, he indicated Viktor outside and studied the Major with his piercing gaze before saying softly: 'And beware of Tartars.'

That night they bumped into the NKVD post on the bridge. As usual it was the General who spotted the place first. Suddenly he reined in the white stallion and indicated that they should do the same.

'What is it?' Viktor whispered, suddenly fearful.

Holding his big hand across the stallion's muzzle to prevent it making any noise, the General answered urgently. 'Up there on the bridge — at the far end. Must be a militia or NKVD road block.'

It took Peter a good ten seconds before he could make out the helmets of the little group of men clustered there, warming their hands around what looked like a brazier. 'Yes, I can see them, General,' he said at last. 'Do you think they're looking for us?'

The Cossack General shrugged. 'I don't know — and besides it doesn't matter.

'We've got no identity documents and nothing to explain why we are still wandering about so long after curfew.'

'Well, what are we doing hanging about here?' Viktor demanded, anger replacing his fear. 'Heaven, arse and twine, man, let's be off before they spot us!'

'Where do you suggest we go?' Alexei replied calmly. 'I know this area like the back of my hand. There is no other bridge within fifty versts of here and by the time we reached it, it would be well past dawn.'

'We could ford the river upstream, General,' suggested Peter.

'I'm afraid not — the current is too strong for the horses, especially the way they are worn out. No,' he said with a note of finality in his voice, 'somehow or other we've got to get over that bridge.'

For what seemed an age they crouched there, listening to the faint noise of the sentries talking among themselves, their horses trembling at their side, as horses always do when they sense danger or deep water. Then at last the General broke the tense silence. 'My guess is there'll be perhaps half a platoon there — twelve or more. At all events too many for us to tackle without surprise on our side. And we haven't got a chance in hell of achieving any kind of surprise from this end of the bridge. They'd hear us as soon as we placed a foot on it. So.' He hesitated, his face breaking into a cruel smile as the plan began to form in his mind. 'We attack from their end of the bridge — the end they won't expect us to come from, if it is us they are looking for.'

'But how are you going to do that, General?'

'Not *we*, Major. But just I. Now listen.'

His boots were slung round his neck; the muscles of his burly arms screamed with the strain they were being subjected to. Alexei threw himself forward one last time and caught the next spar. His hands, already numb and bleeding from the tremendous effort of swinging monkey-like from rung to rung underneath the bridge, seized on it and held. Thus he hung there for a brief instant, while below the river gurgled menacingly.

Alexei took a deep breath and swung his bare feet forward. They struck something wet. The bank. Carefully he sought a hold. With a soft sigh of relief, he let go of the spar and dropped noiselessly to the ground. Cautiously, his boots still slung around his neck, but with a knife in one hand and the *Natschalnik's* knout curled around his right arm like an obscene snake, all three metres of it, he began to climb the bank.

There were five of them crouched round the brazier, their eyes closed, their rifles resting between their knees as they slept in the red-glowing warmth. To their right there were perhaps another seven or eight of the NKVD soldiers sprawled out asleep on their groundsheets, their rifles neatly stacked at their feet.

Carefully he moved closer to them, uncurling the long black whip as he did so. Thirty metres ... twenty-five ... twenty... Now he hardly dared breathe ... fifteen metres... Suddenly he gasped as a sharp pain shot through his foot. He had stepped on something. He tried in vain to check his yelp of agony. At the brazier, he saw one of the sentries stir uneasily. In its ruddy glare, he could see the man's eyelashes flicker — a sure sign that he was waking up.

The sentry opened his eyes slowly. For what seemed an age he stared at the dark figure crouched there, whip in hand. Then his lips parted. With a grunt Alexei threw the knife. It hissed through the air, silver in the ruddy glare. The NKVD soldier threw up his hands to protect himself, but the knife caught him in the throat. Alexei sprang forward, the obscene whip slithering from his arm as he did so. It cracked once. The neat pyramid of rifles flew apart A fat-faced corporal at the brazier opened his eyes.

There was a crack like a pistol shot as the long leather snake shot through the air. The corporal's face contorted with terror and agony as it wrapped itself round his neck. Next to him, another NKVD man tried to lift his rifle. '*Come — now!*' Alexei yelled at the top of his voice and slashed the diabolical lash through the air once again.

As the clatter of horse hooves and the wild rifle fire indicated that the Fritzes had heard his cry, Alexei dropped the whip and diving into the ditch on the opposite side of the road, started to pick off the survivors with his pistol. Five minutes later it was all over and they were already heaving their bloody and dead victims into the fast-moving stream of water below. Ten minutes later, they had filled the horses' saddlebags with what loot they could find and were galloping south again as if the devil himself were after them.

It was first light. The sun was beginning to rise above the white-tipped mountains of the Caucasus on the other side of the broad river, filling their dark folds with its pink shadows, driving away the tendrils of mist which curled catlike around the distant peaks.

But Alexei, dust covered and tired, astride his sweat lathered mount had not even eyes for the beauty of the faraway mountains which were their destination. His gaze was fixed hungrily on the slow-moving river. 'The Don,' he murmured, 'the Quiet Don.'

Next to him Peter relaxed the reins of his weary mare and allowed her to crop the juicy new grass of the river bank. He stared down in silence at the shallows of the great river. For him the River Don, which barred the way into the Caucasus, meant simply another stage in von Kluge's plan. But for the Cossack the arrival at the river had almost a religious significance. After so many years away, after so many wars, so many strange peoples, so many dangers and vicissitudes, he was back in his own homeland. Although the sun was rising higher every second and time was of the essence if they were going to get across and under cover before it was completely light, he knew he must allow the Cossack this moment.

Next to him, Alexei stared at the water, remembering the golden days of his carefree barefoot youth when he had swum naked in it or attempted to catch the black-bellied fish lazing in its drowsy peace, reaching up idly for the juicy slow flies.

Now he was a mature man, already over forty, who had fought for twenty years for his Fatherland, had gained honours and high rank, had then lost that rank and everything else he held dear and who was now preparing to betray that Fatherland. For what? For revenge? No, he told himself. Because he had fought for the wrong Fatherland. This was his Fatherland and it had taken him all these years to learn that fact. Now he must ensure that it became free as it had been of old and belonged to the Cossacks, with their easy democracy of the *Krug*.

The case seemed hopeless: he, a Red General, a traitor to his own people, trying to make a bunch of half-wild outlaws into a trained military force to restore the power of the Don Cossack horde. But he knew with almost clairvoyant certainty that he could pull it off, and make those men in the far-off mountains follow him to the ends of the earth if necessary.

General Alexei brought his hand down hard across the stallion's rump. 'Come on,' he roared, 'let us not waste any more time, my dear Fritzes. We have a lot to do.' And with that he urged his trembling mount into the water for the long swim to the other side and the Caucasus.

CHAPTER 2

As they rode steadily southwards now, the sun shone perceptibly redder, losing the yellow hue it bore further north. By mid-afternoon its rays made the air shimmer electrically blue and the far-off snow peaks glittered unbearably.

At last they were able to ride on saddles which were pleasantly warm, their jackets flung open, a soft southern wind cooling their faces. Even the horses seem to notice the change in the weather. On the second day after crossing the Don, Alexei showed the two Germans how to tie up their horses' bushy tails Don Cossack fashion so that their mounts' rumps would be cooled by the wind.

The character of the country was also changing. The steppe became more broken, its grass no longer so lush as that they had left behind. The little straw-roofed villages, which they avoided anyway, became fewer and fewer as they started the long climb towards the peaks in which the Cossack renegades and outlaws had their hideouts.

On the fourth day their food gave out and they rode on in silence, listening to the rumblings of their stomachs, all three of them sucking pebbles to quench their thirst, knowing now that they had to ration their supply of water carefully. What surplus fat the two Germans still had on their bodies began to disappear rapidly and once on a halt, Alexei opened his collar to show them the little leather sack around his neck and joked: 'If you have to go I'll give you a little of my earth.'

Peter looked at him curiously and wiped the back of his hand across his scummed, parched lips: 'What do you mean, General?'

Alexei tapped the bag and said, 'Well, you see, each Cossack carries round with him a little bag of earth from the village he was born in. When he dies, his comrades place it in his right hand and bury him like that. So wherever it is they plant his tired bones, they can tell his kin that he was buried in his native earth.' He chuckled softly. 'If you two have to go, I'll ensure you're buried in good Cossack earth and not in this Godforsaken place.'

Viktor looked at him sourly, the beads of sweat trickling down his brick-red face. 'Instead of jokes, what about trying to ensure we get something to eat today... My guts are beginning to do somersaults with hunger.'

On the sixth day, they cleared a hill and, a couple of versts away, saw a fertile green valley, with four wooden huts set in a stand of shady white birch. Alexei frowned thoughtfully, while next to him, Viktor licked his lips greedily, his dark eyes staring at the huts as if he could already visualise the food their larders contained.

'All right,' he said finally, 'I know it's damn dangerous but I can see we've got to eat. We'll go down and see what we can find. All the same,' he flashed Viktor a look of warning, 'we're going to do this like a military operation.' He indicated the birches which ran half way up the hill towards them. 'You two get yourselves into that and work your way down towards the huts, ready to give me cover, if there's any trouble. Once you're in position, I'll ride down there and scout round. To my way of thinking, only harmless peasants could live out here. All right, off you go.'

Peter hesitated. 'Watch yourself, General. At the first sign of trouble —'

'Don't worry, little brother,' the General said, moved by the one-armed Major's concern. 'I'm a born looter. I'll be careful.'

But when the General finally made his reconnaissance, he found whatever danger the group of huts might once have contained had gone — two of them had been gutted by fire, their roofs destroyed, two stone fireplaces standing like rough gravestones over the cold ashes. The other two were still intact, but their contents were thrown about in hopeless confusion as if one of the sudden storms of the steppe had ripped through them at one hundred kilometres per hour.

'What do you make of it, General?' Peter asked, dismounting wearily and staring at the ruined cabins. 'There's been no fighting within kilometres of here. Lightning perhaps?'

'What's that then?' Viktor croaked and pointed a finger, which trembled slightly, at the grisly object which lay on the ground fifty metres or so away.

'By the Holy Mother of Kazan,' cursed the General, 'it's an arm!' He crossed over to it, bent down and gingerly turned the horrible thing. A dull gold star, half-covered in caked black blood came into view. Hastily he dropped it and wiped his hands on the back of his breeches. 'Well, did you see?'

'You mean the star?' Peter asked, his voice still shocked.

'Yes, and you know what that means, don't you?'

The Germans shook their heads.

'That star belonged to a *politruk* — a commissar. So that makes this place a militia or NKVD post.' He pushed his fur cap to the back of his head in the typical Cossack gesture of bewilderment. 'But in God's name, what would anyone want a post out here for? We haven't seen a soul in days.' He fingered the little leather bag of earth around his neck with uneasy fingers. 'Very strange, very strange indeed ...'

They were wolfing down a poor meal of charred potatoes, skin and all, washed down with copious draughts of ice-cold water from the deep well when they got the first indication of why it had been necessary for the Soviet authorities to build a police post in this remote valley.

Viktor stopped in mid-bite, his mouth still full of burnt potatoes, and gulped, 'Look — up there, to the right?'

Alexei let his potato drop to the grass and stared, his big hard body suddenly alert and tense.

Some ten riders, rifles slung across their chests, were walking slowly across the top of the far hill, their outlines silhouetted starkly against the crimson ball of the afternoon sun. He narrowed his eyes against its shimmering rays and tried to make them out. Silent as death, like the ghost-riders of the legends with which Cossack mothers used to frighten their children, they moved purposefully down the hill and it was obvious that their destination was the huts.

'What are we going to do?' Viktor gasped, 'they're coming this way. Perhaps they want water from the well for their horses.'

'Shut up!' snapped Alexei savagely. He knew he had to make a quick decision. The strange riders were armed with rifles and they had only three automatics between them. It would be purposeless to attempt to make a stand in the huts. They had no food to make a stand anyway. He hammered his big fist against his knee in sudden rage. After coming all this way, he was not going to let himself be stopped by a handful of police militia, who probably didn't know one end of a horse from the other. 'Listen,' he said urgently, 'we're going to make a run for it — they're going to see us in a few minutes anyway.'

'I agree General,' Peter said grimly. 'But which way?'

'The only way — through them. If we ran back the way we came they could pick us off at their leisure as we tried to get up the hill. No, that's out of the question. As soon as they're down here, we go for them. Surprise will be on our side at least. You,' he snapped at Viktor, 'give me that stake over there!'

The SS Major thrust the metre long stick into Alexei's hand. The Cossack grasped it and tested its weight. It would do. 'All right, on your horses the two of you. Check your automatics and keep close to me. When we hit them, don't bother to take aim, just fire into the bastards and then go hell-for-leather for those trees up there on the far hill.

'We should be in the trees before they recover from their surprise,' he hesitated for an instant, 'and if anybody gets hit, no going back for him. Is that clear? All right, stand by. Here they come!'

They could see the riders clearly now. All of them wore wolfskin jackets with the fur on the outside so that their shoulders seemed immensely broad. Their legs were clad in shiny knee-length leather pantaloons and untanned yellow leather boots. But although their appearance was highly unmilitary, their rifles were definitely not peasant sporting guns. They were the latest issue Red Army weapon. Alexei told himself hopefully that perhaps they were some local collective farm group acting as an auxiliary patrol. But whatever they were, they looked dangerous. They were spread out in a rough line with a short fellow on a great dark bay cantering a couple of lengths ahead. That would be his man. Knock him out and with luck it would take the strange riders even longer to recover from their surprise. Then he would veer left and bolt for the trees. Alexei gripped the stake more firmly in a palm that was already wet with sweat. 'All right now!'

The stallion leapt forward, his white ears pressed flat against his head, his neck quivering, his long mane streaming. On his back Alexei was seized by the old elation. All fear was gone along with reason, logic, coolness, as the desire to kill overcame him.

Suddenly the strange riders spotted them. Here and there a man fumbled with his rifle. But it was their leader on the big bay who reacted first and with surprising swiftness. He dug his spurs into his mount's flanks, urging the bay into a gallop, his sabre gleaming wickedly in the blood-red rays of the sun.

Behind Alexei the two Germans started firing at once. One of the riders clapped his hand to his shoulder and slumped across his saddle. Another cursed in agony and dropped to the ground. But the wild burst of fire did not deter the man on the bay. He came on until the two leaders were only a matter of metres apart.

Alexei clenched his teeth as he came in for the kill. Opposite him the other man raised his sabre swiftly, the gleaming blade clenched firmly in his right hand. Alexei's heart missed a beat. The other man had reacted just as he thought he would. He tugged at the reins slightly to move the excited stallion to the left so that he could strike with the stake in his right hand. The other man did the same. Now he was leaning slightly to one side with his sabre ready to strike.

At that moment Alexei pulled the old trick which had seen him safely through a dozen cavalry mêlées. With all his strength he tugged at the bit so that the stallion broke sharply to the right. In a flash he threw the stake from his right hand to his left, thanking God once again for the fact that he had equal dexterity with both hands. He caught a glimpse of eyes full of shocked surprise under bushy black eyebrows, set in a dark bearded face before his stick cracked down on the other's face. With a cry of agony, the man let go of his sabre and fell from his horse, caught completely off guard by the old 'Baklanov' sword trick which Alexei had learned from his father as a fourteen-year-old. Then the three of them were through the other riders and galloping madly for the cover of the trees. They had nearly reached safety when the stallion put a foot in a marmot hole, sending Alexei flying to the ground. Groggily he tried to rise to his feet, vaguely aware of the two Fritzes reining their mounts ahead of him in the red mist. He tried to wave to them to go on, but somehow or other, he could not move his hand. Stupidly he knelt there, attempting to fight off the blinding nausea.

'I've got the bastard! ' said a voice that seemed to come from a long way away and the brass butt of a rifle slammed sickeningly into the nape of his neck.

Alexei grunted with pain and rolled to the ground, still semiconscious. Men were galloping and shouting all around him, but the noise did not seem to matter much any more. A coarse, tough face seemed to be towering above him. He saw the gleaming butt of rifle being raised into the air and then a grotesquely distorted hand push it aside. He caught a swaying, shifting glimpse of a dark bearded face with a red weal running across one cheek, and heard a voice say: 'Don't hit him again. Only a Cossack could use that damned Baklanov trick...' Then the red mist swamped him and he saw no more.

CHAPTER 3

Alexei lay on the ground in front of the huts. He tried to open his eyes. But when he did, he could not see anything. For one horrifying moment he thought he had gone blind. Then he realised that the thick, heavy sweaty object which covered his face was his own fur hat, thrown over his eyes to protect them from the sun's rays. Feeling something like a sharp red-hot prong being thrust into his right eye as he moved, he pulled the hat away and tried to look up. He groaned and let his head fall back painfully. For a moment he lay there, not daring to move before he attempted it again, this time very slowly.

A line of sweating trembling horses with shaggy wolfskins thrown over their gleaming flanks came into view by the fence. Next to them one of the two men they had wounded knelt awkwardly, his bloody shirt ripped down to the waist, while one comrade washed out his wound with water from the well and another prepared a mud and leaf poultice to cover the flesh wound. Alexei watched the man pour the sparkling, ice clear well water over the wound and licked his caked lips; at that moment he would have given his right arm for just one handful of the clear fluid, and both for a bucketful to dip his splitting head into.

He groaned again and carefully turned his head to the right. The two Fritzes, their faces gleaming with sweat in the midday heat, were tied — tethered might be a better description — to one of the stone chimneys by a long rope of the kind Cossacks had once used to hobble their horses where the grazing was poor. His heart sank. Why hadn't the fools taken his advice before the charge. He cursed softly and checked to see if he

102

had been tied in a similar fashion. To his surprise he found he hadn't. He licked his parched lips and asked aloud, 'Why?'

'Why what?' said a soft voice above him, while a dark shadow blotted out the sun.

Alexei narrowed his eyes painfully and looked up. It was the man he had knocked off the bay with the old trick. Now he stood there, a compress held against his injured face, staring down furiously at his prisoner with bold black eyes.

'Why I was such a damned fool as to let myself be caught like that. Anybody but a fool should have watched the ground. There was always the danger of marmot holes near trees.'

The other man with the black Kuban fur cap set on the back of his curly hair nodded sympathetically. 'For someone who knew the old Baklanov trick like that, it was a nasty oversight, I agree.'

'Did I hear you say the Baklanov trick?'

The other man nodded.

Alexei's heart skipped a beat. 'Then you must be a Cossack, little brother!'

'Yes I'm a Cossack,' he replied, unmoved. 'And don't "little brother" me, prisoner.' His dirty hand fell to the big automatic at his hip. 'There are Cossacks and Cossacks, you know?' he said slowly and menacingly. 'And up in these mountains, only one kind of Cossack survives.'

Alexei licked his lips again, knowing that his own life and that of the Fritzes depended entirely on the response to his next few words. 'You mean … perhaps,' he said carefully, 'those Cossacks who owe allegiance to General Kulakov, eh?'

The stranger's hand dropped from his automatic. 'All right,' he snapped, 'you'd better spit it out. Who in three devils' name are you?'

At last the General had finished his account of his escape from the camp and explained the reason for their presence in the mountains; then he leaned back against the wall of the hut and waited for the other man's reaction.

The bearded man with the weal, who had introduced himself solely as Gregor, nodded and flashed a look at the two young German officers, gorging themselves on cold porridge. 'Fritzes eh?' he said finally, his dark eyes wary. 'Three months ago I was fighting against them myself.'

'You were in the Red Army?'

'Yes, General, I was a staff captain with Lev Dovator's Twentieth Cossack Corps.'

Alexei laughed. 'Lev Dovator — I know him well. He was with me in Poland in '20. How is he?'

The other man's face remained sombre. '*Dead,*' he answered dourly. 'Shot and left to die on the ice at Ruza last December because those swine of the *Stavka* in Moscow let the Cossacks bleed themselves white to make up for their own stupid mistakes.'

'What do you mean?' Alexei asked, sensing the other man's bitterness.

'Mean? I mean the same thing happened once again, as has been happening all the time since we went to war against the Fritzes and our little Father in Moscow took over the direction of our operations.'

'Stalin?'

'Yes, our dear little Father from Georgia who makes one mistake and compounds it by making another. So what happened on the Ruza? He orders a frontal attack by cavalry across rough ground to capture back a few versts of worthless territory which we had lost through his own stupidity. The result? Ten thousand Cossacks dead or seriously wounded without even making a dint in the Fritzes' position — and General Dovator, the most capable cavalry commander in the Red Army left to die by himself on the ice. His life thrown away for nothing, betrayed as we Cossacks have always been betrayed by those in Moscow.'

'Ay, ay,' agreed several of the bearded ragged outlaws.

'That was enough for me,' Gregor continued. 'First I got drunk. Three whole bottles of pepper vodka. Then I hit the Corps *Politruk* — he had naturally been the one to transmit the order for the little Father. Then I drank some more, cursed Stalin, the *Stavka* and was working my way through the marshals of the Red Army from Klem downwards when the NKVD came to arrest me.' He shrugged. 'You can guess what happened then, General, you've been through it yourself?

'First the bastards beat me — I passed out twice. But that wasn't enough for them. Oh, no! They stripped me naked and dropped me in the privy. Up to my neck in the shit, I was. Then they paraded me in front of the *Politruk* — the one I punched — and told me to take back what I'd said about the little Father. Of course, I did. How can a man be a hero without his clothes and covered in shit, I ask you? They let me go after that. I was posted to a punishment battalion and the first opportunity I got, I was over the hill.' He took a deep breath and tried to control his rage.

'That's why I hate the bastards like I do. And that's why I'm here with this bunch of rogues, plundering, raping, burning wherever we can find the bastards and their women. That's what happened to this place. We took it on our way and killed the local commissar. We were going to spend the night here on our way back to the mountains.'

'What is the situation up there — er, Captain?' He added the rank deliberately, guessing that Gregor was not completely happy with the company he was keeping and was missing the discipline of the Cossack Corps.

'They're a bunch of rogues as I've already said. Some of the older men, who've been up there since the defeat of the White Army have settled down with their women to become farmers. But the younger men have no interest in farming.' He shrugged. 'Some are genuine political cases, who fled in the thirties because of the persecution of the Cossacks. Then there are Red Army deserters like myself — and some are simply bandits who prefer to kill and rob rather than work.'

Alexei absorbed the information for a few moments. Then he spoke. 'Listen, Gregor, I'll put my cards on the table. Your General Kulakov made his way across to the Fritzes because he thought Hitler would come and free the Cossacks.'

'Yes, I heard about him.'

'But it isn't as simple as that. Their Führer won't come and free us. We will have to free ourselves!'

'How do you mean, General?'

'That bunch of deserters, outcasts and bandits will have to be organised into a fighting force — and quickly.' Alexei hesitated. 'And then they will have to be led into action against the Red Army.'

Gregor whistled through his teeth. 'General, have you had your hundred?'

'No, Gregor, I'm perfectly sober. We've got to show the Fritzes that we are prepared to shed our own blood to gain back our old freedom.'

'I understand, General. But it won't be easy with this bunch. Most of them don't know the meaning of the word discipline.'

'Then we'll have to teach them it, won't we?' He thrust out his hand. 'Gregor, will you help me? I need good officers.'

Gregor took the hand and pressed it spontaneously. 'General you can count on me.'

Two days later in the golden light of the spring morning, harnesses jingling, scattering the dusty chickens, the little group cantered towards the small, straw thatched, white painted collection of huts, which made up the first outlaw village. Already the first blue wisps of smoke were emerging from the *isbas*' primitive chimneys and as they came closer to the village, the soft clop-clop of their horses' hooves in the dust started the lean, skinny ribbed dogs lolling outside the huts, barking. People began to come out, alarmed by the noise. Heavy built, kerchiefed women, followed by gawping, barefoot, shaven headed boys who stared open-mouthed at the newcomers. Old men, dressed in bits and pieces of the traditional Cossack garb, unlit pipes in their mouths, peered into the rising sun trying to make out who they were.

'Your men, General.' Gregor leaned forward over the neck of his bay and whispered, 'Take a good look at them. They're a fine bunch, eh?'

Alexei's hard gaze rested on the young men for a moment. They were indeed 'a fine bunch': scruffy, unkempt, eyes bloodshot, boots unpolished, with the look of men about them who lived solely for the next drink and the next woman until finally they were fortunate enough to be carried off for good by a stray bullet in some obscure skirmish or other. 'Yes, I see what you mean, Gregor. But at least they're Cossacks — that's what counts.'

Gregor shrugged. 'I hope you're right, General.'

General Alexei concentrated on making a proper entrance into the outlaw village. He knew his Cossacks — they were great gossips. Within hours his entrance here would be going the rounds of the other villages. He reined in the stallion with a great flourish, and staring around at the assembled peasants, demanded in a parade-ground bellow: 'Where is the *Starosta*?'

A shaven headed boy sped away to find the missing headman, while a heavy-breasted peasant woman came forward shyly, bearing the traditional gift of bread and salt. The General took a piece gravely as Cossack custom demanded. But he neither thanked nor spoke to her. His first words had to be reserved for the headman.

The *Starosta* was an old man with a long wispy white beard, his feet bare and his skinny legs protruding from his skimpy white cotton trousers. He stared up at the imperious figure towering above him silently on the white stallion, and touched his trembling old hand to his forelock in the Czarist sign of respect. 'Who are you?' he said. 'Your name, *gospodin*?'

Alexei waited for the full attention of the crowd before beginning to speak: 'My name is Alexei — *General*,' J he emphasised the word, 'Alexei Bogdan.' An excited whisper ran through the crowd. Alexei pretended not to have heard it; his lean, handsome face remained set in stony indifference.

At his feet the *Starosta* waited till the crowd had calmed itself again, then he looked up at the General seated motionless and impassive on the horse. 'And why have you come into these mountains, your honour?' he asked.

Alexei raised himself high in his stirrups so that the young men at the back of the silent expectant crowd could see him clearly and hear every word. 'Because Cossacks — men and women — I have come here like Stenka Razin and Bogdan Kkmelnitski once did so long ago to raise the black flag of revolution, to lead you all in these mountains on a march for freedom. Major,' he swung round suddenly on Baron von Kranz, 'read them their General's letter!'

Peter was prepared for the request; they had planned how they would do it the night before. He unfolded General Kulakov's letter from Berlin and read it out to the gaping villagers.

Alexei hardly gave them time to absorb the General's words. 'You see, your old Commander is now in Berlin with the Fritzes. He can no longer lead you, but I can!'

'But to what purpose, General?' asked one of the young men. Alexei glanced imperiously at him. 'To what purpose? I'll tell you... *V perjodi ze osvoboshdenije rodini*!'

The old cry struck home. Caught up in a wild Cossack enthusiasm, the whole village roared back the words: 'FORWARD TO THE FREEDOM OF THE HOMELAND!'

BOOK TWO: *THE BATTLE OF THE TURKISH RAMPART*

'We'll need every man we've got before the next two days are over. Tartar Hill is a key position. The enemy will attempt to regain it at all costs.'

General Alexei Bogdan, May 1942.

THE CAUCASUS, APRIL 1942

CHAPTER 1

Those first days of the spring of 1942 in the Caucasus were beautiful. Every morning the blue sweep of the sky above the snow-capped mountains was filled with the dark V formations of the wild geese flying north to the cold, while their replacements, the sun-loving cranes, floated gently downwards, heralds of the heat to come.

New life came with dramatic overnight suddenness. The steppe below turned from a pale to a dark, lush green, the poplars lining the steep approach to the village blossomed with their sticky, scented buds and the willows bordering the rushing, still ice-cold mountain streams were green and laden with new catkins.

And just like the sudden onrush of the spring, the news that Alexei had arrived in the mountains spread from village to village, passed by word of mouth to even the remotest mountain fastness.

Day after day Alexei rose at dawn, poured a pail of icy cold water over his dark hair, grabbed a piece of new bread baked by the widow with whom the three of them lived and swung himself on to the saddle of his stallion to begin a new day of conferences and planning in the mountain villages. Late at night he would return, red-eyed, exhausted and hoarse from talking so much, but with another handful of recruits to his cause. To Peter von Kranz, bored with his own lack of activity, it seemed that the tall Cossack general with the tough adventurer's face had been saving all his energy in those long years in the concentration camp for just such a task as this. The Cossack had thrown overboard all his reservations about the dangerous operation; now, it seemed, that he was out to convince every last bandit and Red Army deserter that the only way they could ever achieve a real Cossack way of life again was by following him.

The mountains were abuzz with excited talk of a *Krug* in which Alexei would be elected as the first Hetman of the Don Cossacks for over twenty years — the first Hetman since the failure of the White Revolution, who would raise the black Cossack flag of insurrection once again. The young Cossacks who had thrown in their lot with Alexei lived as recklessly as had their forebears of the great days, loving violently while the hours spent away from their sweethearts were filled with excited, heady talk of the coming revolution against the 'Reds'; the older men, who had settled down to farming after fleeing into the mountains, sat drinking vodka under the shady trees, talking and boasting of old battles and past glories until they slid in a drunken stupor to the ground.

The first of their sons, immature farm boys, started riding into Alexei's village to be trained in the old art of Cossack warfare by Captain Gregor and the little squad of ex-Red Army men he had organised to give some discipline to Alexei's followers. The little bearded Captain would exercise the red-faced slow farm boys on their lumbering horses for a day at a time, drilling into them the rudiments of cavalry fighting.

'Let the enemy come at you from the right,' he bellowed, dark face streaming with sweat from the vigorous demonstrations he always gave, 'then when he's about twenty metres away and leaning to one side and ready to strike with his sabre, do *this*!' Like magic his gleaming curved sword hissed through the air, the sun's rays sparkling on its steel blade, and landed in his left hand. 'Now swing your horse sharply to the other side and go like hell for his undefended side. Believe me,' he touched the now healing weal on his own cheek, 'it works! Now come on, you clod-hoppers, let me see you try it!'

Time and time again, he forced them to practise the quick switch of hands till their arms ached and their hearts pounded. But he had no mercy on them until at last they could run the gauntlet of the twin lines of saplings, cutting off their tops at full gallop, flinging their curved swords from one hand to the other, as if they had been doing it all their lives. Only then did he allow them to dismount and pour buckets of icy cold water over their sweat lathered, crimson faces.

More and more men, most of them little more than bandits, poured into the village. They didn't take to the new discipline like the farm boys and the older men, but after a few of them had had a taste of Gregor's iron fist, they decided it would be easier to accept orders than another 'bunch of my dirty big knuckles', as Gregor called his justly celebrated fists.

Already in the villages sworn to Alexei's cause, stocks of lead were being melted down to make bullets for family fowling pieces or ancient World War One vintage Mauser rifles dug up from beneath their latrine hiding places in back gardens. The older men and their smooth-faced sons showed off their prowess proudly to the grinning outlaws armed with their captured Red Army weapons, though as Gregor remarked ruefully to General Alexei, after they had watched one such group fire a volley of sizzling, half-melted homemade bullets, 'God knows if they'll frighten the Red Army, General, but I do know that they frighten the britches off me! That's for certain!'

Ten days after they had arrived in the mountains, the two German officers, freshly washed and shaven, were sitting on the little wooden porch outside the widow's *isba*, savouring the evening cool and smoking *Marchoka* cigarettes, when they heard the excited clatter of hooves down the village street, and saw Alexei's white stallion emerge from the velvet gloom. The General reined the sweating horse to a sudden halt in a cloud of dust and dropped lightly to the ground.

'I've done it,' he cried excitedly to the Germans.

'Done what, General?' Peter asked lazily, throwing away his cigarette.

'I've decided to call the *Krug* — the day after tomorrow in that big meadow outside Novocherkassk village. Gregor and his men are spreading the news now. They'll come from all the villages.'

'Good, good,' cried Peter von Kranz. 'I agree it was time. Soon we've got to be on our way.'

Alexei became thoughtful. 'Yes, Major, that is what I wanted to talk to you about. There are two things I must discuss with you. I think I've got a goodly number of them with me, especially the older men and their boys. But I'm not so sure about all of the younger ones and it is exactly them I have to convince. But with what am I going to convince them? After all, most of them have been little better than bandits for years now. All they respect and understand is power. What power have I — except my own bare hands and my brain?'

'I don't quite follow you, General?' said Peter, while Viktor sat silent and moody, apparently fully occupied with his homemade cigarette.

'I want to show them — the waverers, the doubters, the unconvinced, that is, that General Alexei, the new Hetman of the Don Cossacks, has more than just talk behind him. More, he has the power of the German Army as well. Now listen, this is what I want you to do for me?'

'Impossible,' Viktor objected when he had finished. 'The time is too short till the *Krug*. Besides, where would the

Luftwaffe find sufficient planes with a long-distance capacity to get this far at such short notice.'

Alexei ignored him; by now he knew that the dark faced SS officer would sabotage any attempt he or any other Russian made to do some independent thinking. The one-armed blond Major was different, however. He really was passionately interested in the Cossack cause. 'Well, Major?' he asked. 'Will you do it for me?'

'I'll give it a damn good try, General. I'll talk to my people by radio immediately.' He rose to go, but Alexei caught him by the arm.

'There is one more thing. The mission itself. I think the time has come for you to tell me exactly what you want me and my Cossacks to do, if I can convince them to follow me the day after tomorrow.'

But before Peter had time to answer, Viktor cut in brutally, a sneer on his dark face. 'You know where the Parpach Isthmus is, don't you?'

Alexei nodded.

'Well, it is planned that you and your Cossacks will attack the rear of the Red Army holding the Parpach position, which blocks the German Army's passage into the Caucasus. That's what the German High Command wants from you, Cossack.'

If Viktor had expected some sort of outburst of surprise or fear, he was disappointed.

'Is that all?' Alexei said mildly. 'Some four thousand Cossacks, armed only with small arms, to attack the rear of a whole Soviet corps, dug in in positions which have held you off for three months.' He shook his head gently. 'Is that all?'

Peter von Kranz opened his mouth to say something, but the General indicated that he should not speak. For a moment there was silence, broken only by the hoarse cries of the cranes nesting in the high reeds outside the village.

'I shall do it,' he announced finally. 'What other course of action lies open to me anyway? I am a fugitive, a traitor, a man caught up in a fast flowing river that will probably take him to perdition.' His harshly handsome face twisted momentarily into a bitter smile. 'But no matter, I am prepared to struggle so that I don't drown this day. I want to live a little longer. Yes, I'll do it, Fritzes. But I make one condition.'

'Condition?' snapped Viktor and flashed Peter an urgent glance.

'Yes. If I can convince the Cossacks to follow me at the *Krug* then I'll do it. If I am successful and your forces can occupy our old home the Don Basin, then you must allow us to return there' — he paused for a second so that they could be quite clear about the full implication of his demand — 'and give us the opportunity of establishing an independent Cossackia, as of old.'

'Peter,' Viktor cried in German, 'remember the Reichsführer's attitude to Russian political aspirations!'

'*Ach, halt die Schnauze,*' Peter snapped harshly. Solemnly he rose to his feet and extended his one hand to the General. 'General Alexei, on my word of honour as a German officer, I promise you that my superiors will ensure your demands are met if this operation is successful.'

Alexei took the outstretched hand and pressed it hard. 'Good, Major. Thank you. I'll remind you of your promise when the time comes.' He yawned suddenly. 'Now I'm going to bed — there's a lot of work still to be done in the morning and you'll want to talk with your people no doubt. Good night.'

'Good night, General,' Peter said, while Viktor glared at the Cossack in naked hate.

As Alexei passed inside the *isba*, he caught a glimpse of his face in the widow-woman's cracked, flyblown mirror. It was the hard face of a man who had been burdened too early with too many responsibilities: the face of a soldier. Now it was all starting all over again. Could he pull it off — could he really make a success of the impossible mission? Swiftly he pulled himself together. Of course, he could. Hadn't he pulled off similar crazy missions in the past? As he sat on the rough and ready bed, unwrapping his foot rags from feet that had suddenly begun to ache, he told himself that now everything depended on the *Krug*.

CHAPTER 2

The spring sun had been beating down mercilessly since the early morning. The meadow outside the village of Novocherassk, (where on St Peter's Day the outlaws celebrated by drinking themselves into insensibility) shimmered in the blue trembling heat haze. The sky had turned a heavy leaden grey, shrouding the copper ball of the burning sun. There was a hint of a storm in the heavy, electric air.

But the thousands of Cossacks assembled there, their faces flushed a deep crimson with the heat and vodka did not seem to notice the unseasonal weather. They stood in excited chattering groups, holding their sweat lathered horses with one hand, the other clutching a glass of vodka or a mug of black tea and honey, thick and as tacky as glue, discussing the outcome of this first *Krug* in over twenty years. And all the time more and more of them came riding in on their shaggy ponies, some of them bearing the silver sabres which had been handed down from one generation to the next for centuries, to be greeted by the catcalls of those already assembled on the big meadow.

Alexei was seated on an upturned saddle underneath a withered crab tree with Gregor and his squad and the Germans. He watched the excited scene apparently unmoved. For his harsh lean face betrayed none of his inner tension. If he did not succeed in being elected Hetman at the *Krug*, there would be nothing left but to become an outlaw like the bunch of wild young drunks sweating in leather jerkins at one of the long wooden tables groaning under the weight of buckets full of vodka, which they drank straight from the pail.

Next to him Major von Kranz was equally anxious that Alexei should be elected this boiling hot April day. But his grim face revealed the inner tension. He looked up continually at the leaden sky and prayed that the threatening storm would hold off until the Luftwaffe had played its role in the coming election.

In front of the long tables, the village headmen started to assemble. Some of them were younger men, proudly wearing captured Red Army uniform, their belts crowded with looted automatics. But mostly they were ancient wrinkled Cossacks, wearing carefully brushed *Cherkesskas*, heavy with the silver and gold medals they had won at Peremyshl, Warsaw, Lvov and even earlier battles at Geok Tepe and Sandep.

'Cossacks,' one of them stammered in a thin voice, 'attend me!' Then he turned to the blond youth with a kettle drum standing next to him. 'Give them a roll on the drum, boy — sharp!'

The rattle of the drum had its effect. Slowly the chattering and the drinking ceased and silence descended on the Cossack host assembled on the burning steppe.

Under the crab apple tree, the little group tensed. Slowly, well aware that thousands of eyes were watching him, General Alexei rose to his feet and pulled his *Cherkesska* straight. He nodded to Gregor whom he had chosen to be his lieutenant in the old Cossack fashion.

The ex-Red Army staff officer, chest ablaze with decorations swung himself easily on to the bay and trotted slowly towards the headman, bearing aloft the traditional Cossack horsehair standard. Behind him came Alexei on foot; his cap under his arm in a sign of respect that custom demanded. Slowly, the red-faced sweating crowd parted to make a lane for the two of them, their eyes fixed curiously on this legendary Cossack

General, who had once betrayed them to fight for the Reds, but who now wanted to raise the black flag of revolution against his former masters if he were elected Hetman.

Peter von Kranz, standing next to Viktor, watched him stride forward purposefully, towering head and shoulders above most of the crowd, and realised that he was watching a man of destiny. At that moment, the Cossack seemed somehow to express boundless self-confidence and the conscious superiority of a man fated to lead a nation.

Alexei reached the headmen. He made a stiff little bow to the grave-faced men assembled there and waited in silence. But the crowd were still mumbling among themselves and although the senior headman held up his arms for quiet, they continued to talk; they were too excited and in some cases too drunk.

Alexei's face darkened. Suddenly he sprang on to the headmen's table and swung round to face the crowd. There was a gasp of surprise. Alexei clapped his hands to his slim hips and glared at their sweating faces. 'Cossacks,' he yelled, 'when I was a barefoot boy, my father told me if I ever had to make a speech, I should stand up, speak up — and shut up. Now I'm going to do exactly that.'

There was a burst of laughter at the sally, but it died when the onlookers saw that the grim look had not vanished from Alexei's face.

'Cossacks, I want you to elect me as your Hetman, according to our old custom, but before you do, I'm going to tell you a few hard truths. A long, long time ago we Cossacks did a great wrong when we helped to put down the 1905 Revolution. We have long memories of our own revolutionaries, our Razins and the rest, and so have the Russians. For the last twenty years they've punished us for 1905. They have taken away our lands, they have taken away our uniform, they have even taken away the very name of our country.'

'Ay, ay,' came a thunder of agreement from the crowd.

Alexei's voice rose. 'For twenty years now we have suffered indignity after indignity. But the time has come to put an end to them. And for the first time since 1920, we have the power in our hands. Not too many versts from these mountains, German soldiers are preparing to drive into our old homeland. They come not as our enemies, but as our *allies.*'

'That's what you say, Alexei,' called a cynical voice from the group of young drunks.

The General ignored it. 'Over one hundred years ago, our old Count Platov, Hetman of the Don Cossacks, not only saved Russia from its enemies, but also freed the Germans of theirs. Now those Germans are to return the compliment. They will free us, Cossacks. But we must help them. We must do our share.'

'You lie Alexei,' the drunk called.

'Who said that?'

'*I did!*' A huge Cossack of about thirty with a grey lambskin cap at the back of his head pushed his way through the throng. He planted his booted feet firmly apart and glared up at Alexei, squinting into the sun's glare. 'And I'll tell you more, you are a whore Alexei, earning your wages in the Fritzes' bed. The old days of the Cossacks are over. Anybody but a fool knows that. We can only survive if we stay up in these mountains where the Reds can't get at us. Besides I don't trust the Fritzes. I fought against them on the Bug last summer before I deserted and I know them. They treated our prisoners like pigs. Look,' he ripped open his shirt to reveal the swastika branded on his chest, 'that's what some of their SS boys did to me before I escaped. I say we stay here in the mountains.'

Alexei stared down impassively at the man, although his brain was racing. The man and his tangible proof of the German attitude were having their effect. 'All right if I'm a whore, then you're a tame lap dog, happy with the scraps you can beg or steal from those peasants down there on the plains. You're wearing britches, so I suppose you're a man, so why don't you show some courage like one.'

'What did you say?' The big Cossack's hand dropped menacingly to thee automatic stuck loose in his belt.

'You heard me,' Alexei said softly.

'Listen, *General*, all you'll do is bring down blood on the heads of the Cossacks to no avail. That's why somebody's got to stop you.'

'You're a coward,' Alexei said coldly. 'Coward!'

'What?' The Cossack's face flushed purple. His big hand tugged at the automatic. But at the same moment, Alexei shouted: 'Gregor — *sabre!*'

The Captain's sabre flew through the air. Alexei caught it expertly and a second later the Cossack screamed piercingly, as the gleaming blade cleaved his skull. There was a sudden hushed intake of breath, followed by a scared silence, broken only by the metallic sound of Gregor thrusting his sabre back into its scabbard.

'Cossacks,' Alexei said abruptly, 'today, you have to make a decision. You have to decide if you want me as your Hetman to lead you to fight with our German friends against the Red Army. In return, if we are successful, we shall regain our lands and our home.' He raised his forefinger in swift warning. 'But do not be mistaken, Cossacks, it will not be an easy life. We shall have to give up the safety of these mountains and those of you who have families will have to leave them behind. Undoubtedly Moscow will try to stop us before we ever reach our objective. Cossacks, as your Hetman, all I can offer you is hope. Now what is it going to be?'

But before they could react, their attention was caught by the faint pulsing in the western sky. Thousands of eyes swung upwards as the pulsing became a trembling and the trembling a steady hum.

At the edge of the crowd, Peter nudged Viktor and breathed, 'Great crap on the Christmas tree — they're here! Thank God — Fat Herman and the Luftwaffe have come through!'

The roar of the planes grew louder. The gaping throng could now make out the individual planes, eighteen of them flying in a perfect V formation.

Suddenly one of the young men saw the black and white crosses on the three-engined transports' corrugated metal sides. 'Fritzes!' he yelled in alarm.

'Don't panic,' Alexei yelled from the table. 'They are our friends, you will see.'

But it was obvious that the crowd of Cossacks didn't quite believe him. Some of them hunched and prepared to throw themselves on the ground, as soon as the bombs began to fall. They had all learned to have a healthy respect for the Luftwaffe in these last few months.

Slowly the two squadrons of Junkers 52 transports came lower. The tense expectant throng could see the white blobs of the pilots' faces in their cockpits and the crews throwing open the side doors. Alexei nodded to the two Germans. They ran quickly to the long arrow of grass they had fashioned beyond the crab apple tree, pointing to the empty field that had been picked for the DZ. Peter von Kranz lit a match and threw it into the grass, jumping back swiftly as the blue gasoline flame shot along the arrow, turning it into a huge directional sign. A second later the first of the dark shapes hurtled from the plane.

'Look out, Cossacks!' someone yelled in fear. 'Bombs!'

The crowd scattered wildly, pushing at one another frantically in a sudden panic. But the dark objects' rapid descent was being halted by the sharp dry crack of parachutes opening. The crowd stopped in their tracks, hearts beating furiously, not quite knowing whether to trust the evidence of their eyes: red, white and green canopies sailing slowly and gracefully downwards, bearing their cargo of brand new automatic weapons for the Cossack horde.

A group of young men raced for the first long metal container and kicked open the catches excitedly. One of them reached inside and pulled out a Schmeisser machine pistol, the magazine already attached. 'Look,' he yelled crazily and pulled the trigger. White tracer zigzagged furiously into the leaden sky.

'You see,' Alexei cried, as the amazed Cossacks watched package after package come floating down, as the Junkers came in for their final run before turning westwards once more. 'Did I not say that we had powerful friends in Germany — friends who will not let us down, as they have just shown!'

Suddenly the sultry air was full of the excited voices, which drowned even the roar of the Junkers, '*Elect him … elect Alexei as Hetman…*'

CHAPTER 3

The great trek westwards started three days later. At dawn.

During the night, in the mountain villages, the barns and stables had vomited forth their contents: ancient high-bridled pony traps; great lumbering canvas roofed farm carriages; ancient once elegant, pre-Revolutionary traps that had lain untouched under two decades of dust; stout, four-wheeled handcarts towed by a wooden handle — anything that would move on wheels.

And into these carriages the old men who were going with them packed their food supplies, the bedding and the heavy machine guns which the Fritzes had dropped over the meadow. Then they assembled in their village squares ready to move.

Meanwhile the younger men were not idle either. They began forming up with their tough mountain ponies laden down with grain (their basic ration), their bedrolls and their weapons into rough and ready village squadrons, awaiting Alexei's orders. As the sun started to slip over the horizon, colouring the dirty white of the sky a glorious red, the orders came through: wagon train to move off, flank guards out to protect them.

The still morning air was full of the sounds of snorting horses, the hoarse cawing-cawing of the alarmed rooks, the harsh cries of the riders and the wailing of the women and children who were to be left behind. The old men set off grimly, driving their carts through the lines of howling women, throwing up their white shawls in front of their contorted, tear-stained faces, blowing their noses on the hems of the white calico underskirts. But the young men, tugging at their bits so that their mounts pranced on two legs dramatically, shouted boastfully to their girlfriends and mistresses what they would do with those 'little turds of Reds' once they got within striking distance.

On a height overlooking the rough road that led out of the mountain fastnesses, Alexei, surrounded by his escort from Gregor's Red Army deserters, watched them stream out of their villages like the Cossack hordes of old. Despite their lack of discipline, their shabby ponies and even shabbier clothes, they looked good to his trained soldier's eye. With surprise on their side, they'd do it. But first they had a long and difficult trek in front of them.

'Well, General Alexei?' Peter von Kranz asked. 'What do you think of them now?'

For the first time since he had come into the mountains, Alexei's lean face broke into a semblance of a smile. 'A rabble, major, a definite rabble. But the best irregular cavalry in the world, as you are soon going to find out.'

TO THE CRIMEA, MAY 1942

CHAPTER 1

A Russian patrol first spotted them on the afternoon of the second day of the trek west. Gregor and the General at the head of the riders protecting their right flank, reined in their sweating mounts and focused their binoculars. Before them the limitless steppe seethed in a brown heat haze and Alexei could see how the very thin air above the parched grass trembled with it.

'Cavalry,' he announced after a moment's scrutiny, 'a good dozen of them.'

'And from the NKVD by the look of them,' Gregor added grimly. 'Those bastards.'

'What now, General,' asked Peter von Kranz anxiously.

'Nothing. We will wait and see how the situation develops.' Stuffing his binoculars in their case, he raised himself in the saddle and yelled: 'Forward at the walk.'

The trek continued but as the afternoon passed leadenly, with the two Germans casting increasingly frequent looks at the horizon and a translucent grey mist started to veil the brazen sun, more and more enemy cavalry appeared on their flank, tiny black wary figures keeping pace with the Cossacks.

Alexei did not allow them to halt and take up a defensive position until evening. Finally with the dark shadows sweeping across the steppe from the east like the flight of gigantic night birds, he gave the order to dismount in between two shallow gullies, adding that the old men should go about preparing the evening porridge and bacon, as if everything were quite normal.

Alexei wiped the sweat from his face, burnt a leather brown by the sun during these last two days and turned to Gregor. 'We must play Cossack games with them, Captain. We must test them out, find how serious they are about tackling us. What their strength is. What else is to come.'

'Don't talk in riddles,' Viktor snapped irritably, his whole body aching from ten hours' solid riding. 'What do you mean exactly General?'

'I mean those men out there presume we are ignorant Cossack outlaws — more than would normally go out on a rampage from the mountain hideouts — but still people who have no idea of warfare. So what do such people do when they meet an enemy? They dig themselves in, form a barricade on the nearest bit of high ground and wait to see what happens.' He rubbed his lean unshaven jaw thoughtfully. 'The old fallacy of high ground and defence.'

'So what do we do?'

'What they expect us to do — we barricade ourselves in on the high ground up there.'

'What!' Viktor exploded.

'Well, not exactly my Cossacks.' He turned to the nearest old man. 'You, little father, what's your name.'

'Boris, your honour.'

'All right, Boris, I want you to get together a hundred of your old chaps and get them up on the hill up there with spades. And this is what I want you to do. Dig in up there and make it obvious that you're doing so. Let the enemy see you at work and as soon as it gets dark light a few fires — take some of that animal dung you have with you, there's no wood up there.'

As the old man hastened away to carry out Alexei's command, the General turned to the others. 'As soon as it's dark, they'll attack. And when they do, we'll be waiting for them — over there in that patch of wood at two o'clock. It's obvious that they'll use it as their cover to get as close as possible to the hill without being spotted. And one final thing. I want only one single prisoner — for information.'

Gregor laughed drily and spat into the dust. 'No survivors, General, eh?'

'No, Gregor, no survivors. So see that you have men wide out on the flanks to ensure that when the shooting starts, none of them bolt and attempt to go back the way we came. We want to keep the fact that Cossacks are on the march again secret as long as possible. We're going to live longer that way.'

A thin mist writhed between the trees as they pushed through the hushed forest in single file, each rider of the two hundred Cossacks Alexei had selected for the ambush picking his way along the narrow trail with the utmost care. They passed a long dead cow, slumped on its back in a ditch, its legs sticking up stiffly from a grotesquely swollen belly. Here and there a horse's whinny was stifled by a hasty rough hand over its nostrils; the NKVD cavalry could not be more than a couple of versts away now and in the evening stillness sounds carried a long way.

A stream barred the way. Alexei, who was leading the Cossacks personally, held up his hand for the column to stop. The horses would make a lot of noise going through the water. Somehow he must cover that noise. For a moment he peered through the trees. Then he spotted what he sought. Letting his Cossack knout slide down his wrist like a thick black snake, he cracked it suddenly. Almost immediately hundreds of rooks rose from the trees cawing hoarsely. At the same moment the Cossacks spurred their horses forward, springing and splashing through the stream as best they could before the noise of the birds had died away.

Five minutes later Alexei ordered his men to halt. They spread out swiftly in a long line, hidden in the trees that bordered the trail through the forest. Behind them on the hill, the old men would have already lit the fires now so that the NKVD would think they had dug in for the night. Alexei touched the little leather bag of earth around his neck to reassure himself that it was still there as he always did before he went into action. The minutes passed leadenly as they perched there on their mounts in the grey gloom, nerves on edge, ears straining for the slightest sound. Nothing.

Then they heard them. A snatch of whispered hurried conversation down the trail. The rattle of metal against metal. The sharp muffled cough of an impatient horse. The NKVD cavalry.

'Draw sabres!' The whispered command went from man to man.

Silently the Cossacks gripped their weapons in hands suddenly wet with sweat. They all knew how much depended upon their wiping out the NKVD cavalry. If even one of them managed to escape and alarm his headquarters, the Red planes would be out searching for them before dawn and on the open steppe, a bombing attack could result in a bloody massacre.

Now, on the shifting wind, they could hear the soft shuffle through the dust of many horses' hooves. The NKVD were advancing on the hill beyond in full strength, confident obviously that they would take the Cossack position without difficulty and then roll up the long convoy of wagons in the valley in a matter of minutes.

'Here they come,' someone whispered at the end of the long line of Cossacks, 'a whole lot of the bastards!'

Alexei tensed. Staring down the trail, he could see them quite distinctly now. A double line of riders, outlined against the mist, as they bounced up and down on the backs of their horses. Slowly Alexei began to raise his sabre. He controlled the stallion which was beginning to tremble violently as it scented the danger to come. They were only a matter of metres away now.

'*Attack, Cossacks!*' Alexei's urgent cry split the silence.

Gregor next to him, jerked the trigger of his pistol. A stab of violet flame. A NKVD man screaming in sudden agony. One of the riders slumping in his saddle and starting to slip from it with dramatic slowness. Then the Cossacks charged full tilt into the NKVD. The silent glade was transformed into a chaotic scene of murder and mayhem, with men screaming and falling as lead hissed through the air like heavy summer rain. Horses reared and plunged, snorting with fear. At the head of the ambushed column a young officer was on the grass screaming for a mother who was far away as the first Cossack horses galloped over his writhing body and put an end to his misery.

Alexei hurtled towards an NKVD officer, his gold stars clearly visible in the silver rays of the newly risen moon. The officer tugged fearfully at his pistol and fired wildly. The slug hissed by Alexei's head giving the Cossack time to raise his sabre and bring it down with one swift vicious slash through the NKVD officer's skull.

Alexei tugged at the bit and swung the stallion round. A white, crazed face loomed up in the middle of the cursing, sweating, struggling throng of riders, now pivoting and prancing on the moaning bloody bodies of those who had already fallen. The General caught a glimpse of red-rimmed, burning eyes and lips drawn back over yellow, foam-flecked teeth before he swung his sabre again. The red-rimmed blade whistled through the air. The NKVD man fell screaming over the rump of his horse, head cleaved to the jaw.

Alexei crashed into a throng of sweating bloody riders hacking at each other, swirling round and round in a mêlée of rearing frightened beasts, cracking pistols and flashing bloodstained steel. In their midst a young Cossack crouched, his arm cut off at the elbow while an NKVD man was about to bring his sabre down on his defenceless head.

Alexei was too far away to reach him in time so he used the old Cossack trick in a mêlée. Drawing back his arm he threw the sabre like a spear. It went right through the NKVD soldier's body, its point appearing between his shoulders. As Alexei reined his sweat lathered, trembling mount, reaching down to pull out his bloodstained sabre, the one-armed boy gave him a wan smile. 'Thank you, General.'

The Cossacks were murdering the survivors of the NKVD cavalry with systematic cruelty. They were forcing them into increasingly tighter circles, and hewing them down as if they were a gang of crazy butchers, hacking and slashing, plunging and gouging, chopping and cutting until the whole trail lay littered with dying horses and mutilated bodies.

Then one by one they dropped from their steaming horses. Some just lay there among the dead, too weak to move. Others began to loot the dead.

Half an hour later Alexei had completed his interrogation of the sole survivor, a handsome young giant whose broad chest was decorated with the Red Star and the Order of the Soviet Union. At first he had refused to talk, but Gregor's knout lashed across his pale face a couple of times, turning it into a spider's web of dripping blood, had soon changed his mind.

Apparently ever since Gregor's raid into the valley a couple of weeks before, and his murder of the Commissar, the NKVD had been out looking for the outlaws. Indeed Headquarters had finally agreed to send a whole battalion into the field to look for them.

'Did your commander radio his HQ this afternoon that he'd spotted us?' asked Alexei.

The prisoner answered in the negative. The headstrong NKVD Major, his skull now split by Alexei's sabre, had decided to wipe out the Cossack bandits and then claim the victory later.

Alexei leaned forward in his saddle and clicked his bloodstained fingers excitedly. 'Did you hear that Major von Kranz? We might have another twenty-four hours — if we're lucky — before the Reds learn that we are still alive.' He nodded to Gregor. 'All right, Gregor, he's yours.'

Gregor's Cossacks, their eyes sparkling in the thin silver light, needed no urging. Some of them had twenty years of old scores to pay off against the secret police.

Viktor tried to intervene: 'General, you can't let them take him.'

Alexei stared at him harshly. 'It's the Cossacks' revenge for the past,' he said. 'They must have it for the thousand indignities they have suffered these last twenty years. Besides, now there is no way back for them. They have committed themselves irrevocably this night. Now we must win — or die — because they'll hunt us to the end of the world. The die is cast!'

It was only after they had blinded him that the Cossacks, eyes bright, staring and fanatical, ripped open the prisoner's trousers and pulled out his proud masculinity. A sabre whistled through the air. The prisoner screamed one last time, as they stuffed his genitals into his mouth and slashed the sign of the Cossack across his dead face.

Two hours later, with a soft yellow full moon warming the steppe in front of them and clearing the mist, they began to ride westwards once more. Behind them the wood lay full of dead men stiffening slowly in the night air. The front line was less than thirty-six hours away.

CHAPTER 2

They rode all day. The brazen heat was heavy with the sweat of horses and men, and the warm leather smell of their saddles: verst after verst with no sound save the dry throated commands of the drivers, the creak-creak of their wagons and the stolid plod-plod of the animals through the steppe.

Time and again, at Alexei's command, the cavalry on both flanks swept out in great fanlike movements, throwing up huge clouds of dust as they cantered off in search of the enemy. But the steppe was empty. It seemed that the Cossacks ploughing steadily westwards were alone in the swaying burnt green of the feather grass.

But in spite of the burning heat and the exhaustion of both man and animals, Alexei kept the trek going, until finally, long after darkness, he allowed them to stop with the warning: 'No fires tonight, Cossacks, and cold rations... The front's too close now!'

Most of the Cossacks, parched and exhausted from the long day's march, contented themselves with pouring a pail of blessed water over their burning heads, swallowing a handful of cold white beans and a piece of greasy bacon and then throwing themselves on to the hard ground to fall into a heavy sleep.

But for some reason, Peter von Kranz could not sleep. He tossed and turned on his bedroll with his saddle as a pillow, listening to the soft shuffle of the sentries and staring up at the silver sparkle of the stars and what the Cossacks called the 'little sun'. And somehow his own unease was reflected in the behaviour of the horses, which kept snorting fretfully and jerking every now and again at the long ropes which tethered them near their masters.

Next to him Viktor threw back his rough horse blanket and groaned softly. 'What is it?' Peter whispered. 'Can't you sleep either, Viktor?'

Viktor shook his head. 'Though I should be able to. I'm dog-tired. It was one hell of a day.'

Peter yawned too. 'Yes, I know. But there's something in the air. I don't know but I feel somehow that they're out there, looking for us.'

'You're right, Peter. I've had that feeling all evening.' Viktor started abruptly as a horse snorted at a night shadow. 'Listen,' he said suddenly, 'Peter, let's make a break for it! We've done our best for these brutes. Let's get out while we've still got a chance. After what happened yesterday, the NKVD won't leave one man jack of us alive. They'll slaughter the lot — with pleasure.' He grabbed the other officer's hand in a paroxysm of fear. 'Peter, what do you say?'

Peter von Kranz tore his arm free and in the same moment brought it back and slapped the SS officer across the mouth. 'Now listen, you cowardly bastard, we're not going to abandon these people. Our treatment of the Russians has been bad enough ever since the campaign began. Now we've actually managed to convince a goodly number of them to fight on the side of those who tortured and abused them and you want simply to abandon such people when the going gets tough. In heaven's name, what kind of asparagus Tarzan are you, man?'

But his contemptuous question was drowned by the sudden drone of motors. The small blond hairs at the base of his skull sprang up. In a flash, Viktor's cowardly suggestion was forgotten. Suddenly very wide awake, he stared up at the silver blue sky, already knowing what he would see up there. Far, far to the east of the silent camp, a small black shape, silhouetted against the stars was getting larger with every second. 'Ach, by the great whore of Buxtehude,' he cursed angrily. 'A Soviet recce plane ... the bastards have found us again.'

They moved all night, hurrying north-west in rapid flight, urged on by an anxious Alexei, while the droning *Yak* and its successors followed their terror-stricken progress over the steppe, with flare after flare, bathing them time and time again in their icy, unreal light.

Once Alexei, trying to throw the damned recce planes, led the column into a long stretch of pine forest. But the road through it turned into little more than a track, bordered on both sides by deep ditches full of brackish water and mud which the spring sun had not yet dried out.

The going got tough, very tough. Often the old men driving their supply carts allowed their vehicles to plough into some deep puddle. A wheel would crumple and suddenly the little shaggy pony drawing the cart would be treading air wildly, fighting for the security of the track, while the cart would be swinging inevitably towards the flooded ditch.

In a flash the narrow track would be blocked. The exhausted Cossacks would lay into the mud-caked, shivering pony, already frothing at the mouth with fear and effort, trying to force it free of the mud. Time and time again, with back-breaking regularity.

And Alexei would be everywhere, tearing up and down the long stalled column on his sweat lathered stallion, pleading, urging, commanding, threatening, lashing both horses and men with his knout until finally the column would start moving yet once again.

Just before dawn when most of the Cossacks had nearly reached the end of their tether, Alexei ordered them off the track into the woods, leaving their stationary carts camouflaged with leaves and branches, while yet another two-engined *Yak* droned somewhere overhead in the ugly white pre-dawn sky trying to discover their whereabouts.

Peter von Kranz slumped down wearily among the pines next to a flushed Gregor, his chest still heaving wildly after helping to push a cart out of the mud for the tenth time, his boots mired to the calf. The bearded ex-Red Army staff officer was in an ugly mood, and for some reason he found it necessary to take his rage out on the weary German sprawled on the wet ground next to him.

'Do you know, Fritz,' he snapped without any preliminaries, 'you think this is hard. But last year when your troops attacked us without warning, I saw things that no one in his right mind would believe possible.'

'What?' Peter croaked and stared at the Cossack's angry face. 'What did you say, Gregor?'

'You heard,' the bearded Cossack growled and wiped a dirty hand across his sweating brow. 'When they caught our partisans on the Bug, they stripped them naked and popped them, hands tied behind their backs, into water up to their necks. Within the hour they had frozen into blocks of ice. That's what you Fritzes did last year. But that wasn't the only mistake you made. When you marched into the Ukraine, the peasants received you as friends — liberators and not conquerors. But what did you Fritzes do? You turned them into little better than slaves. Our women — virgins or not — were stripped naked in front of your medical centres like a bunch of poxed-up whores to be examined as to whether they were fit enough to be exported to your holy Reich to work in your factories on starvation rations. Why, I ask you, Fritz, did you do such things. Why?' He glared challengingly at Peter, who was bewildered by this sudden attack.

'*Why?*' Alexei's harsh voice cut into the conversation. 'I'll tell you, you horse's arse! Because the world's full of fools like you, Gregor, who ask the right questions at the wrong damn time. That's why! Instead of sitting there, shooting off your big stupid mouth, Gregor, try to use your brains — if you've got any — to find a way for us out of this mess.'

'I meant no offence to our German comrades, General.'

'All right, all right,' Alexei growled. 'As long as you realise that it is not only the Germans who are a terrible people on occasion. We're not much better. Yesterday was a good example of what I mean. Save your energy for finding some way out of the trap we're in.' He jerked a thumb at the sky in the direction of the drone of plane motors. 'Otherwise pretty soon that bastard up there is going to bring the whole weight of the Soviet Air Fleet down on top of us. And believe me, brothers, that is not going to be very pleasant.'

But when they emerged from the forest half an hour later, the Red reconnaissance plane was still there, droning round in steady, irritating circles to the east, obviously radioing their position to its base. A group of angry Cossacks loosed a volley of fire in its direction. But the *Yak* kept up its observation of their progress westwards in sovereign disregard of the bullets winging harmlessly in its direction. So they rode on towards the pink horizon disturbed here and there already by the bright red flashes of the heavy guns at the front.

An hour later, the cavalry flank guard to the right, breasted a low hill and saw below them the sprawl of a typical eighteenth century village of the area, with beyond it the buildings of the new collective farm built in the thirties. The news was reported to Alexei at once. He urged his horse into a gallop and rode with his escort to survey the place.

The village seemed deserted. Although the collective farm workers should have been up and about their work hours before, the place was strangely silent; and there was no smoke coming from the peasants' *isbas*.

'What do you think General?' Gregor asked.

Alexei replaced his binoculars thoughtfully in their brown scuffed leather case. 'I'm sure there's somebody down there. Look there are horses tethered there at the side of that big white barn. If the villagers had fled, they would have taken their horses with them.' Alexei fumbled unconsciously for the bag of earth around his neck. 'If the villagers are in hiding down there, it must mean that they are loyal to the government. Does that sound reasonable to you, Gregor?'

'Yes, General.'

'And if they are hiding down there, instead of having fled, it must mean, too, that they are prepared to defend themselves. Further, that they are in touch with the authorities, yes?' He looked at the bearded captain. 'So, if we attacked them and they defended themselves, it could well mean that our feathered friend up there,' he indicated the *Yak* recce plane, 'could well have the bombing attack postponed until the pilot knows what the outcome of our little battle might be.'

'And?' Viktor butted in, his face a mixture of fear and anger. 'What then in hell's name? Sooner or later they're going to send in the dive-bombers to wipe us off the face of the earth.'

Alexei did not look at him. 'We shall play games with the defenders of the village until nightfall. Then if we are still alive by that time, we mount up and ride like hell through the Red Army's second line and if we are lucky enough to surprise the rear echelon troops, we take up our positions on the Turkish Rampart.'

'The what?' Viktor, Peter and Gregor cried in surprise.

Alexei swung his stallion round to the west. 'Can you see that shimmer? Well, that's the Black Sea. Now to the right of the shimmer, can you see that dark line running across the hills?' He pointed his dirty forefinger at what looked like a ditch running across the horizon, its outline trembling in the morning heat. 'That's the Turkish Rampart. The Turks built it long ago to keep out the Tartars. It's a wall of earth running right across the Perekop Isthmus, some fifty kilometres behind the front. I know it well from the old days of the Civil War. Now where it approaches the coastal road, it covers the road and the sea with a man-made hill — the *Tartar Hill*, the Turks called it. It's some five hundred years old, but all the same it's a damn good defensive position, comrades, especially when it is held by determined men who have nothing more to lose,' he hesitated momentarily, 'than their lives.'

CHAPTER 3

The morning was furnace hot. The steppe quivered in a blue haze. The glare cut at the watchers' eyes, as they followed the little patrol's progress towards the silent village. There was no sound now save for the anxious coughs of the nervous ponies of the wagon train down in the gully and the faint drone of the reconnaissance plane.

Slowly, strung out in a long, careful line, the Cossacks' horses started to wade through the long grass, with the sun beating down on them fiercely, making their flanks gleam with sweat. They were about three hundred metres from the silent village, Alexei calculated, watching them through his glasses. If the village were defended, the firing would have to begin soon.

A bustard started up beneath the leading horse's hooves. It reared in alarm. Alexei started and cursed his own nervousness, as the bustard sped away, its white under feathers flashing as it rose swiftly into the blue haze. The lone riders cantered on, their pace quickening now.

There was a sudden flash of light to the east. The watchers swung their heads round as one. It was the *Yak*, using its signal lamp. They tensed, while the little patrol rode stolidly on.

Suddenly they heard a single dry crack like a brittle twig being broken underfoot. One of the Cossacks clapped his hand to his shoulder and began to slip from his horse. For what seemed a long time nothing more happened. Then all at once, with an angry rattle, a ragged volley rippled down the length of the front row of cottages. A succession of violet flashes and lead was striking the ground everywhere in front of the

Cossack patrol. Hastily their leader raised himself in his stirrups. His sabre gleamed in the sunlight. '*Charge!*'

The firing from the cottages intensified. Another Cossack was flung from his mount at full gallop. His body bounced twice as it hit the ground. Still the others pressed home their hopeless attack with the wild abandon of their warrior race. A horse screamed in hysterical agony, plunging to its knees and flinging its rider in a crazy arc over its head. He was up an instant later and running after the rest. An ancient machine gun chattered. The lone runner faltered. His sabre slipped from his hand. Slowly his knees crumpled beneath him and this time he fell for good. Then what was left of the little patrol was riding full tilt into an open barn. The hot wind carried the faint snap and crackle of small arms fire to the watchers on the hill.

A minute passed. Five. Still the firing continued. Then there was silence. A riderless horse appeared at the door of the barn, then began to wander aimlessly back across the steppe, stopping every now and again to crop the long grass.

The patrol had sacrificed themselves, as they had known from the start they would have to, and the battle for the village had begun.

It was noon. Out on the hilltop a couple of hundred Cossacks were sprawled out in the grass, their shirts soaked black with sweat in the terrible heat, sniping at the village. Stripped to the waist, Viktor and Peter sheltered beneath a crippled wormwood tree and rapped out their call sign over and over again, while the *Yak* droned round and round in its lazy circles, obviously waiting for the outcome of the battle for the village.

Suddenly the key, far-off in another world, began to chatter with metallic urgency. Peter pressed the earphones closer to his sweating head with one hand and with the other started to scribble down the coded message on the one time coding pad. The stream of morse seemed to go on for ever and in the end, Peter, his finger aching, asked for a break so that Viktor could decode the answer to his initial inquiry about the Red Army defences on the Parpach Isthmus.

As usual Colonel von Tresckow's researchers in Berlin had been very thorough. The twenty kilometre long passage from the Crimea to the Kerch Peninsula was being defended by three Soviet armies — the 47th, 44th and 51st under the command of a Lieutenant General Kozlov. 'Sixteen thousand Red troops per kilometre,' Viktor read in an awed voice. He looked up from the pad and shaded his dark eyes against the sun's glare. 'Man, that's sixteen men per metre!'

Peter absorbed the information grimly. 'And what does the message say about the Turkish Rampart?'

'Fifty kilometres behind the real front. But it's defended ... by a regiment of antitank guns, they think in Berlin.'

'Good and bad,' Peter said half to himself. 'They'll have no infantry cover at least, although we've got nothing that could tackle artillery of that calibre.'

'Perhaps von Kluge could convince the Luftwaffe to help us out?'

Peter's face lit up. 'Of course, I'd forgotten about air support. If Fat Hermann's fly boys could plaster the Rampart before we attacked, it would be one hell of a help. But the main thing is this — when is Colonel General von Manstein's Eleventh Army going to kick off its attack?'

Viktor flashed a glance at his decoding pad. 'It's not here,' he declared after a moment.

'All right, I'll call them again.' Slipping on his headphones and feeling them stick unpleasantly to his sweat lathered cheeks, he started to rattle his key. Ahead of them an old

Soviet machine gun began to chatter angrily again. On the hill the Cossacks' counterfire grew in volume. Peter knew he must raise von Tresckow's HQ in the Ukraine and discover the date of the planned offensive. It was vital, for Alexei's Cossacks could not survive long without the support of regular German troops. Even if they somehow managed to disengage this night, slip through the second Russian line and capture the Tartar Hill on the coastal road, they would need German aid almost immediately if they were going to withstand the enormous weight of the inevitable Russian counter-attack.

The Major managed to get through at last. He posed his questions quickly and signed off. The morse commenced crackling metallically through the ether once more. Hastily he scribbled down a long list of numbers. Almost before he signed off for good, Viktor had begun deciphering them, the beads of sweat dripping in opaque pearls from his furrowed brow on to the pad.

'Well?' Peter demanded impatiently.

Scribbling furiously, Viktor gasped: 'No Luftwaffe for a start. That's out. Every plane is needed to support the Wehrmacht.'

'Ach Christ on a crutch!' Peter cursed. 'And the offensive — when?'

Viktor deciphered the last groups of numbers and looked up, his dark face grim and foreboding. 'On the night of eighth-ninth May,' he announced.

'*What?*'

Viktor nodded numbly. 'Yes. Two days from now. If our tame Cossack General ever does manage to pull it off, he will have to hold out on that hill for at least thirty-six hours against everything those shitty Reds can throw at him.'

'So that's the situation, eh,' Alexei said slowly. 'We'll have to sweat it out on our own for a couple of days, eh? Well, planes or no planes, we'll have to do it. Tonight. Before the fly boys up there in the sky can cotton on to the fact that we are making a break for it.'

'Have you a plan, General?'

'Plan? I wish I had. No, we have no time for fancy tactics now. Time is running out rapidly.' He waved his hand at the far distance, as if he wished to sweep aside the heat haze which obscured the view. 'As soon as it's dark, we'll come in along the beach, below the coast road. Naturally it'll be defended, probably from attack from the sea. But the defenders won't be expecting an attack from their rear, unless those bastards in the sky have warned them what is going on here, but I doubt it. And besides the sand will help to cover up the noise our horses make.' He breathed out hard. 'Our attack will have to be sharp and brutal. And all we can hope for is that with the men available to me we'll be able to roll up the left flank — for a while at least — and take Tartar Hill. You understand?'

Peter nodded automatically.

'However, Major, if we can hold that hill we'll dominate the Kerch-Novorossiysk coastal road which runs through the southern half of the Rampart. That road can offer your armoured forces the quickest route into the Caucasus and at the same time if we can hold it, we can prevent any major supplies or reinforcements reaching the Soviet front once your people have attacked from the Crimea.'

'General Alexei,' Viktor interrupted. 'Aren't you forgetting one thing in all this? How in the devil's name are you going to break away from the fight you've got on your hands already without having the Red Air Force come along and plastering us?'

'We won't break away,' Alexei answered calmly. 'Indeed as soon as it grows dark, we shall treat those Goddamned peasants and militia down there in the village to a full-scale Cossack charge.'

'But where are you going to get the men from, General?' Peter protested. 'You can't afford any more casualties if you're going to tackle the Tartar Hill with any hope of success.'

Alexei put his hand on the German's shoulder. 'You know as well as I do, that this column is heavy in old men and animals. Some of them must be sacrificed to save the majority.' He shrugged. 'It was always the Cossack way — the old must die for the young. And the old men know it. It is a hard decision to have to make, but I am their commander, I shall make it. As soon as we have the cover of darkness, I shall ask the old men who are staying behind to drive the surplus animals towards the village. We'll abandon the carts now, they're only a burden. I hope the animals will kick up enough racket to cover our withdrawal. As soon as we're away, the old men will launch their attack on the village. My guess is that we'll be able to fool the villagers and the recce planes long enough to reach the coast.'

Night came finally, cloudless and windless. The sky was inky black, save to the west where it pulsated with the crimson flushes of the permanent artillery barrage, outlining the stark black silhouettes of the old men smoking their last pipes before driving their animals towards the village.

A mist was beginning to drift in from the sea and as Alexei went from man to man, shaking a hand here, clapping a shoulder there, he seemed to be wading through knee-high grey smoke. Then he swung himself on to his mount and stared down at the old men preparing to make the supreme sacrifice for the rest of them. To his right, Gregor gave a soft order. On muffled hooves, the Cossacks started to move, their eyes staring straight ahead, as if they could not bring themselves to look at the old men for the last time. Alexei hesitated for a few moments. Then he raised his hand to his fur cap in a last salute. 'Goodbye, Cossacks.'

'Goodbye, General,' the doomed men replied in unison, their voices calm, as if they were glad to be quit of life at last.

Alexei dug his spurs into the stallion's flanks and urged it forward. Without a word to either Gregor or the Germans, he took his place at the head of the long column of riders.

Thirty minutes later, when the long column was finally well clear of the battle for the village, an echoing yell rent the inky black silence accompanied by the thunder of many hooves and a few seconds later, a wild burst of panic-stricken firing from the village. The old Cossacks replied with the remembered passion and fury of their youth, as they urged their horses towards the houses. Animals cried out in agony. Men screamed. The firing grew in intensity until it reached a crescendo. The village was outlined by the ugly red spurts of many explosions. Then the snap and crackle of small arms fire began to ebb away, to be replaced by the steady tack-tack of the village's old-fashioned machine guns. In their turn, their bursts grew shorter and shorter until they died away altogether, leaving behind an echoing silence. The last of the old men was dead.

CHAPTER 4

A branch cracked underfoot.

'*Whoreson!*' hissed Alexei. 'Watch your feet, man!'

The young Cossack in front of the General muttered something under his breath, but he stepped obediently enough out of the bushes into the sea glowing faintly in what little light there was. One by one, the advance patrol, led personally by Alexei, followed, wading up to their knees in the still warm water.

'Pass the word,' Alexei whispered, 'watch out for slippery stones underfoot. Anyone who falls and yells out I'll have the eggs off with a blunt razor. Pass the word.'

Alexei waited till the warning had gone down the line of volunteers, then he turned and with his tall lean body crouched so that he could see the outline of the Turkish Rampart high above them more clearly, began to wade cautiously through the water. The men, fingers clenched nervously on the triggers of the Schmeisser machine pistols with which they were all armed, followed in single file.

The minutes passed with no sound now save for their own tense breathing and the soft sigh of the sea. Once a flare hissed into the air. They crouched at once, frozen in its chill light, waiting for the command and burst of machine gun fire. But nothing happened.

'Young soldiers,' Alexei whispered reassuringly to the Cossack next to him. 'Always get jumpy at this time of night.' They pushed on through the water.

All at once Alexei halted and crouched, sniffing the air, his eyes trying to penetrate the darkness of the cliff towering above the patrol.

'What is it, General?' the Cossack next to him asked anxiously.

'They're up there,' Alexei answered. 'That's their first position, covering the coastal road. Can't you smell them now?'

The young Cossack sniffed. 'They smell different from us after five days in the saddle. Garlic sausage and yellow soap. A clean bunch of lads these Reds, eh, General?'

Alexei chuckled softly. 'Well, at least, they'll go to their Soviet heaven with clean faces. Come on.' Without waiting to see if the rest of the patrol were following him or not, he began to climb up the cliff, searching for handholds in the darkness.

A few minutes later they were all sprawled out on the cliff top, chests heaving, fighting to control their harsh breathing, while Alexei surveyed the scene. Finally he spoke. 'You see men, to the left of that clump of bushes there — at two o'clock?'

They nodded.

'Looks like a dug-in antitank gun and to its right, a bunker, I think. God knows how many of the bastards there are in it, but all the same we've got to do the job quick and without noise.'

He drew the sabre that he had hung across his back for the climb. For a moment its curved blade gleamed menacingly in the faint light. 'Sabres and knives only,' he ordered. 'No firearms yet. Understood?'

'Understood, General,' they hissed hoarsely.

'All right, Cossacks — follow me!'

They crawled forward on their stomachs through the damp grass. The stink of horses and the warm, sweeter smell of hay grew stronger. Automatically Alexei told himself that the antitank gun must be horse-drawn. A second later the sound of a fretting horse stamping on a dirt floor and whinnying in warning confirmed his guess. But the gunners, sensing no danger in a position which was so far behind the front, slept on, unheeding the loyal beast's call of alarm, as it sensed instinctively that the crawling figures represented mortal danger. They wormed their way closer. Still no sign that the Reds were aware of their presence. They were only a matter of metres away now from the long-barrelled gun, shrouded against the night damp in heavy canvas.

Alexei gasped in alarm. A youngster with a shock of corn-yellow hair sprang up right in front of him, disturbed in his trench by the sound of crawling bodies. For what seemed an age, the General and the private stared at each other. Then Alexei's sabre hissed through the air and slashed the boy's throat.

They pelted on. Without a word being wasted, two of the patrol dropped behind the antitank gun and started preparing it for action. Another Cossack flung himself flat next to the machine gun which covered the gun.

'What in three devils' name is going on out there?' an irate, sleepy voice demanded. A couple of metres away, a blackout curtain was flung back and yellow light flooded out, while the speaker peered into the darkness uncertainly. 'Who's there, damn you?'

A knife hissed through the air. The officer stumbled back into the bunker, frantic hands clutching the knife stuck in his chest. Someone inside kicked him aside. Another officer, clad only in his underwear, launched himself at Alexei, his big hands searching for the General's throat, his teeth bared in fury.

Alexei tried to cut him down. But there wasn't enough room to wield his sabre on the steps. With a curse, he dropped the sword. His fist smashed into the officer's pock-marked face. Still his hands sought and fought Alexei's throat.

Alexei tried desperately to hit him again, but missed. 'For God's sake,' he gasped to the men behind him, 'Get this bastard off me … I'm choking here.'

A young Cossack behind him reacted at once. His knife flashed: plunged into the officer's back. His big body hunched violently. Blood stained his white underwear. But still he did not let go of Alexei's throat.

'Man, are you never going to die?' Alexei gasped, as the stars started to explode in wild reds and silvers in front of his eyes. 'Finish … finish him off someone!'

The teenage Cossack needed no urging. Springing on to the big officer's back, he grabbed the man's hair and tugged, then with all his strength, the boy sawed his sharp blade across the officer's exposed throat. Alexei swayed back sucking in great gulps of good air, his chest heaving.

Five minutes later the first position guarding the vital coastal road was in Cossack hands at a cost of five dead and seven wounded. Ten minutes later Alexei was signalling to Gregor, commanding the bulk of the Cossacks, to bring up the rest. The attack on Tartar Hill could commence.

It was a night of mayhem and savage murder.

Time and time again little bands of dismounted Cossacks sneaked up on Red Army positions along the vital road like grey timber wolves coming out of the dark forest, slaughtering the enemy while they slept.

All the long night the two sides fought in the warm darkness in thick grunting silence, rifles and machine guns abandoned mostly for bayonets, knives, swords, shovels — anything with which they could hack, slash, cleave. And as the night progressed it seemed as if the road along which they fought was bathed in steaming blood.

But slowly the Cossacks began to gain the upper hand. Bit by bit they won control of the road running through the Rampart so that by the time the first pink flush of dawn appeared in the east, they held it to a length of one kilometre, with their patrols reaching out to a depth of three hundred metres to the east, moving ever nearer to their key objective — Tartar Hill.

Still Alexei was not satisfied with the speed of their drive. Ordering the lightly wounded, who had been collected down on the road, to ready the antitank guns for the counter-attack which he expected from both front and rear, he swung himself on to his stallion and galloped after the lead patrol, heading for the hill, which was commanded by Gregor himself.

After fighting his way through a pocket of Red Army men, who still held out on the road, he found Gregor and his men sheltering under the cover of a group of bullet-pocked trees. Springing from his sweating horse, he ignored Gregor's greeting and flung a swift glance at the squat white barracks which dominated Tartar Hill at the highest point of the Turkish Rampart.

'All right, Gregor, if that place stays in their hands, they'll still be able to dominate the road. We'll have to take the goddam place.'

Gregor nodded, one side of his bearded face bleeding from a sabre slash. 'I thought you'd say that. General... What are your orders?'

Alexei grimly unsheathed his bloodstained sabre. 'No time for elaborate tactics, now, Captain.' He swung himself on the back of his stallion and raising himself in his stirrups so that the Cossacks could see him, waved his sabre. 'Cossacks,' he ordered, 'mount up!'

The exhausted riders clambered back on their steaming mounts, fumbling urgently for their sabres, their eyes fixed apprehensively on the steep slope ahead of them.

Alexei gave them a few seconds to form a rough and ready line of attack. Then he yelled at the top of his voice, 'Cossacks — at the gallop — *Storm attack!*'

Twice the Cossacks charged the hill and twice they were forced back in disorder by the Reds' massed machine gun fire, scattering in panic, leaving the slope strewn with stricken horses and their dead and dying. But Alexei would not give up. Every inch the general, the born leader of men, who knew that his men could break if showed any sign of weakness, he forced them into a third attack. This time they managed to get as far as the southern wall of the fort, a mere handful of survivors, their eyes wide and staring with fear and the strain.

While the Red machine guns poured streams of relatively harmless tracer over their heads, Alexei swung himself on to his horse once more, sabre hanging from the leather loop around his wrist, a captured hand grenade clasped in his free hand. 'All right,' he cried without any attempt to impress the worn-out survivors, 'I'm off. Those of you who think they're Cossacks can follow me… The rest of you who are old women can stay behind and pee your drawers.'

The taunt had its effect on the young men. They flung themselves on their trembling mounts and surged after him.

Alexei shot forward, clinging low to the stallion's flying mane, digging his spurs in cruelly. A machine gun crew loomed up behind a barricade, appearing suddenly out of the fog of war. Alexei pulled out the grenade pin with his teeth then at full gallop, hurled it at the men behind the sandbags. It exploded in a vicious burst of red and yellow flame. Shrapnel hissed — red-hot — through the air everywhere. The machine gunners reeled into the nearby ditch. Alexei's stallion sprang over their writhing bodies.

They burst through the gate into the barracks. Instinctively they split into little groups, riding close to the bullet chipped walls of the big courtyard. The machine gun which opened up from an upper window missed them by a metre. Slugs struck the cobbles everywhere, throwing up showers of harmless blue sparks. Gregor reined in his bay. Without appearing to take aim, he loosed a burst of automatic fire from his machine pistol.

Above him the glass splintered into a crazy spider's web. The window crashed outside, the machine gunner hurtled to the courtyard. He hit the cobbles with a thud, bounced once and then lay still.

'*Inside!*' roared Alexei. He spurred his horse up the broad steps, slashing his gleaming sabre from side to side as he did so, hacking his way through the pale-faced, half-dressed screaming clerks, panicked by the sudden appearance of these wild men in their shaggy furs.

A senior officer raised his pistol. Alexei did not hesitate. He threw his sabre. The officer went down screaming, blood gushing from the left hand side of his open mouth, vainly wrestling with the cruel blade which transfixed him.

After that, the heart seemed to go out of the defenders. More and more of them began to surrender. The trickle became a flood after Gregor had split the heads of three prisoners in the courtyard in full view of those still holding out, yelling: 'That's how we Cossacks can make six out of three of you miserable Artillery bastards! Now are you going to give up — or do we have to come up there and do the same with every single one of you sons of bitches!' Disdainfully he spat on the bloody cobbles and stared up at the survivors, as if daring them to attempt to shoot him.

Ten minutes later the last of them surrendered and the looting of the barracks began. While Alexei and Gregor inspected the place and supervised the disarming of the sullen prisoners, some of the young Cossacks, already guzzling vodka from looted bottles, streamed from room to room, ransacking shelves, lockers, cupboards. As the sun finally edged its way across the horizon, they staggered drunkenly down the body littered corridors, waving their bottles, smashing everything they could not take with them, hauling the boots off the dead, sticking captured pistols in their belts, already weighed down with looted hams and great hunks of ration chocolate.

Then they discovered the women, cowering in the clerks' quarters in ashen-faced fear. 'Field mattresses!' a freckle-faced Cossack yelled in delight. 'Come on boys!'

A female captain, with close-cropped hair, her earth coloured uniform blouse stretched tight over a massive bosom tried to stop them. 'You Cossacks are pigs,' she began. Her words ended in a scream as they picked her up bodily and started tossing her up and down, heaving her ever closer to the high ceiling. 'Now!' the boy with the freckles ordered. She hit the ceiling, smashed the light bulb and then hurtled to the ground with a tremendous crash. 'That'll learn yer, you old mare!' someone yelled exuberantly. 'Now come on, let's see what you've got in that blouse of yours!' The Cossack reached forward and with a grunt, ripped open her blouse.

His example set the others off. Suddenly the whole room was full of the screams of the frightened women and the hoarse animal grunts of the Cossacks, who whenever they met any resistance simply slapped the unfortunate woman into submission. 'Fornicate and be merry!' the old Cossack cry went from mouth to mouth. '*Fornicate and be merry!*'

It was thus that Alexei and Gregor found a group of young Cossacks as they entered the top floor. Naked save for their boots and fur caps, four of them were sprawled drunkenly over a screaming girl, two holding her feet, one her head, while the forth was trying to penetrate her wildly writhing naked body.

'*Yo tuoyu mat!*' the gross Russian obscenity escaped Alexei's mouth at the sight. Then he bellowed: 'Stop that at once! '

He attempted to push away the two holding her feet, drinking in turn from a flower vase full of vodka, but they wouldn't be pushed. Alexei's dark face flushed even darker with rage. 'Gregor,' he commanded, 'give me your pistol.'

'But General, it is the Cossack way!'

Alexei did not reply. Instead he held out his hand impatiently for the pistol. Then clicking off the safety catch, he aimed and fired. The rapist's spine arched. He slumped over the girl's heaving belly, dead. Suddenly very sober, the Cossacks swung round to stare at the tall, lean, angry figure of their leader.

'All right, you swine!' Alexei bellowed, 'get your clothes on and get back to your duties, before I shoot the lot of you!'

One hour later Alexei and Gregor had succeeded in restoring order among the men. Those of the Cossacks who were too drunk to understand that the orgy of looting was over, had been flogged unmercifully by Gregor and his escort and dumped in the barracks' horse troughs to sober up. Now the rest were sweating out the vodka in the hot morning sun, restoring the barracks' defences, swinging round the 50 mm antitank guns so that they covered the white gleaming road below in both directions, hastily filling in the gaps in the sandbags of the machine gun pits, heaving out the dead Reds slumped over the machine guns and re-siting the weapons. As the bloody ball of the sun rose higher in the scorching blue sky, the barracks and the road below was a hive of frantic activity, in preparation for the counter-attack.

Alexei, Gregor and the two Germans stood on the wall of the barracks watching the red-faced Cossacks toiling below, then silently they surveyed the burning countryside to the south, the way they had come. It was still silent and peaceful, its calm undisturbed save for a gentle trickle of blue smoke here and there from the white painted peasant *isbas* which dotted it.

'Well, comrades, we've done it so far,' Alexei broke the silence at last, lowering his glasses.

'Yes, and with remarkably few casualties, General,' Peter von Kranz said drily, pointing to the heap of Cossacks below who were to be buried in a mass grave, separate from the Red Army men who had suffered the same fate.

Alexei fingered the little bag around his neck. 'Yes, thank God — we'll need every man we've got before the next two days are over, believe me, Major. Tartar Hill is a key position. The enemy will attempt to regain it at all costs. Now then, Major, this is what I want you to do. Contact your people —'

'You mean physically?' Viktor broke in, seizing at straws. 'Now would be a good time to sneak through their lines to our own people,' his words died away lamely, as the big General looked down at him, eyes full of contempt, shaking his head slowly.

'By radio, Fritz,' he said. 'By radio.'

'Of course, General,' Peter cut in, ashamed of the cowardice, written on his fellow-countryman's dark, drawn face. 'And the message?'

'Tell them we are in possession of over a kilometre of the coastal road and Tartar Hill, which we intend to hold whatever happens on the road. Now from what I know of the situation on this front, your people's most likely point of attack is to the north. You have a salient up there. Now I want you to suggest to your people that in view of the fact that we dominate the road, they change their plan of attack.' He drew a quick rough sketch in the dust with his boot. 'That they come up from the south — here. Tell them we shall do our damndest to prevent any Red reserves getting through to support that stretch of the front, once the German Army has broken through.'

'One question, General. I think the first question Colonel-General von Manstein will ask himself before he makes any changes in his plans is how long you will be able to hold out up here?'

Alexei opened his mouth to reply, but before he could do so, angry red lights winked all along the southern horizon like a series of blast furnaces suddenly springing to life. Below, the peaceful valley quaked frighteningly. And with a hoarse scream the first heavy shells sped into the blood-red sky, starting their murderous flight towards the defenders of the road.

THE TURKISH RAMPART, MAY 1942

CHAPTER 1

'*Na. Herr Generaloberst,*' asked Sergeant Fritz Nagel, Manstein's driver, with the cheek of his long-established position, '*was meinen Sie?*'

'What do I think, Nagel?' Manstein straightened up from behind the periscope with which he had been surveying the Soviet defences on the other side of the water. 'I think the Ivans will give us a bloody nose, if we're not very careful. That's what I think, Nagel.'

Nagel, who had been Manstein's driver since 1938, grinned in his usual careless manner. He knew that while he had been wounded several times driving the Colonel-General, Manstein himself had escaped without a scratch; that was why the burly clever Army Commander regarded him as sort of good luck talisman. The Sergeant waved his big paw easily in the direction of the silent Russian front on the other side of the Isthmus, bristling with tank traps, gun emplacements, complicated and deadly machine gun nests. 'That bit of scrap iron over there won't stop you, sir. Not more than an hour or two at the most. Shit in the wind, *Herr Generaloberst,*' he added confidently. 'We've got other things behind us, haven't we, sir?'

Manstein smiled and adjusted his gold-braided general's cap. 'I wish I had your confidence, you old rogue. Well, come on let's get back to the staff.'

In single file, heads ducked slightly in case there were any of the Red Army's first-class female snipers about, they marched down the length of the 114th Artillery's observation post and joined the staff waiting behind the cover of the Regiment's command HQ.

'Well, sir?' asked Major General Haccius of the 46th Infantry Division which would lead the assault, a little anxiously. 'Which is it going to be now?'

Manstein pursed his thin lips thoughtfully, swaying up and down slightly on the tips of his gleaming riding boots. 'As I am sure you are well aware,' he began, 'the Isthmus front has a curious shape. The southern end here runs dead straight to the north. But at the northern end of the front there is a big bulge to the west — due to the running ability of our loyal Romanian allies.' He paused for laughter.

It came in polite, subdued tones, as befitted the elegant staff officers. All of them knew how the 18th Romanian Division had taken to its shabby heels the previous winter when the Ivans had attacked, fleeing a good eighteen kilometres in their panic and leaving behind a large salient which German troops had only managed to seal off with difficulty.

'Now, *meine Herren*, the obvious thing would be to attack somewhere along that salient, cutting off the exposed Soviet flank. But that is exactly where the *Stavka* expects us to launch our attack. My opposite number over there Lieutenant-General Kozlov has two of his three armies in that area and most of his reserves too. Naturally our friend from the steppes will be waiting for us there — bless his simple Red soul!'

There was a polite titter from the elegant officers.

'Naturally we shall encourage him, gentleman, to continue in that belief. As some of you already know, I have ordered a great deal of activity in that area in these last few days, plus heavy radio traffic. But, *meine Herren*, as they used to say when I was a boy — everything which glitters is not gold.' He winked solemnly.

Behind the officers Nagel chuckled heartily and muttered something about the 'old man' being a 'right old sly fox.'

Colonel-General von Manstein, the victor of France, allowed the information to sink in. Then very formally, his smile gone, he announced: '*Meine Herren*, my Eleventh Army will attack the Forty-fourth Soviet Army on the southern flank. That is my decision.' He held up his soft hand, as if he expected some sort of protest from the assembled officers. 'Naturally I know all the difficulties and dangers inherent in such an undertaking — a frontal attack on prepared positions — devilishly strong positions at that — and across water to boot. But gentlemen, I have one little trick up my sleeve. Just before zero hour, sappers and infantry of the Bavarian One Hundred and Thirty-second Infantry Division will land on the Black Sea coast east of Feodosiya and —'

But the Colonel-General never finished his sentence. From behind the Soviet front a sudden roar swamped his words, as far away to the east a whole brigade of 'Stalin Organs' crashed into action. Instinctively several of the staff officers ducked. But this time no red-hot steel splinters from exploding shells came their way. Instead the rocket barrage seemed to descend upon a spot somewhere deep behind the Russians' own lines.

'*Grosse Kacke am Christbaum!*' Manstein cursed, his eyes full of sudden surprise. 'What in the devil's name was that?'

For a moment no one answered, then the representative of von Kluge's staff, portly, red-faced Colonel von Tresckow cleared his throat and said, 'Colonel-General, that is the second little trick you have up your sleeve.'

Von Manstein spun round on him. 'What did you say, Colonel?'

'We on the Field Marshal's staff have laid — er — a little egg in the Popov's nest.' Swiftly he explained the basic details of Operation Cossack, while von Manstein listened with ever-growing interest.

'Do you mean to say,' von Manstein snorted when he had finished, 'that over there, those Cossacks of yours have seized part of the Turkish Rampart?'

'That barrage would indicate they had, sir,' von Tresckow said quietly. 'Now sir that's why I am here. From our information we know this Cossack General, Alexei Bogdan, can only hold up against a two-front Soviet attack for twenty-four hours at the most?' He licked his suddenly dry lips. 'Colonel-General, can't you bring forward the date of your own attack one day? I can assure you that Field Marshal von Kluge, my chief, would not object in the slightest.'

Von Manstein shook his big head. 'Not even God could convince me to alter the date of the attack now, von Tresckow.'

'May I be so bold as to ask why, sir?'

Manstein stared down at him through the monocle which he often affected on such occasions. 'For the most obvious of reasons, my dear Colonel. Because our Führer Adolf Hitler has set the date of this attack personally. And I am sure he would not deign to alter it for the sake of a bunch of half-wild Cossacks under the command of some escaped convict, even if his name is Alexander.'

'Alexei.'

But the Army Commander did not hear. He touched his fingers to his cap, his face suddenly icy, '*Meine Herren, ich empfehle mich*,' he snapped. 'Nagel, get the car — at once!'

The staff officers clicked to rigid positions of attention, hands glued to the gleaming peaks of their caps, as the Colonel-General passed through their ranks towards his grey camouflaged Horch. A minute later, he was gone, leaving von Tresckow staring forlornly at the blood-red horizon which somehow seemed to symbolize the plight of General Alexei and Peter von Kranz.

Ten kilometres further east, Lieutenant-General Kozlov, his broad Slavic face flushed with both anger and worry, was at that very moment making preparations for Alexei's 'bunch of half-wild Cossacks' to be wiped off the face of the Soviet earth. The General had no illusions about his own fate if he failed Stalin.

While sweating, anxious staff officers hurried back and forth in the big echoing operations room, he personally telephoned commander after commander and repeated the same simple order: 'Colonel — or General — attack immediately without regard to losses. I want that stretch of road taken before nightfall this day. You understand? If you don't succeed, you'll answer to me for it — with your head.'

Finally he smashed down the field telephone, his barrel chest heaving, the sweat running down his broad face. Swiftly he applied some more powder to his face and dabbed it from the great bottle of cheap Crimean cologne which all the staff officers used in summer, or when fear started to make them sweat more than usual.

'Well, Kuznetsov?' he barked at last at his Chief of Staff, 'what is the situation now?'

Colonel Kuznetsov placed his well-manicured varnished finger nail on the big situation map. 'They've taken about a kilometre of the road here, penetrated to a depth of three hundred metres here.' He hesitated. 'And our latest reports show they've got Height 532 — the Tartar Hill. I'm sorry, Comrade General.'

The General swore. He knew the position well. Indeed, although it was so far behind the line, he had personally ordered it to be fortified because of its commanding position and control over the vital road. 'Shit, shit, shit,' he cried, hammering his big fist on the desk. 'But who — by the Holy Mother of Kazan — are the sons of bitches?'

The Chief of Staff consulted the slip of paper he held in his soft white hand. 'Cossacks, Comrade General, Don Cossacks.'

'But my dear Colonel, how can a bunch of hairy-arsed reactionary shit Cossacks seize a strategic height just like that one which could be decisive for the whole future of my southern flank?'

'They're no ordinary bunch of Cossacks, Comrade. They're commanded by the renegade Alexei, who broke out of the camp a month or so back.' He lowered his eyes discreetly; the General himself had been released from a similar camp himself only six months before, so that he could go to the front.

'That bastard!' Kozlov breathed. 'Him!'

'Yes, Comrade General, that Cossack bastard.'

The Army Commander reached out for the big bottle of cologne and poured a generous slug of it on to his lace handkerchief. Hastily he mopped his brow with it and heaved a long sigh. In his youth Kozlov had been a lieutenant in the Imperial Cavalry; he knew his Cossacks. Most Russians thought of them as bold, careless riders, strong in attack, weak in defence because of the very nature of their tactics on horseback. He knew different.

The Cossacks were cunning, stubborn, defensive fighters who, once they had taken up a position, would not let go of it until they had been beaten out of it feet-first, one by one, like their damned borzoi hunting dogs, whose teeth had to be prised apart before they would let go of their prey. And the fact that the renegade Alexei was commanding them would make the task of defeating them doubly difficult.

'All right, Kuznetsov,' he snapped, pulling himself together, 'what is the situation?'

The Chief of Staff flashed a hasty glance at his watch. 'The softening up barrage will end in approximately thirty minutes. At that moment, the Guards Tank Brigade will attack from the north. You have already talked with their commander —'

'And from the south,' the General interrupted him. 'I don't want any half-arsed measures, you know.'

'You won't get them, Comrade General. I can promise you that. When the Guards go in, the Cadets will come in along the road, supported by fighter cover.'

For the first time that morning, General Kozlov's face brightened. 'Ah, Stalin's Scholars,' he said, using the Red Army slang name for the élite of the Soviet forces: the officer cadet battalions. 'Well, if anybody can pull it off, they can.'

Kuznetsov drew himself up proudly to his full height. 'Comrade Stalin once declared, General, that no fortress on earth can withstand the Bolshevik storm. Our men are that storm, General, they will pull it off all right.'

General Kozlov was not impressed. Once again he dabbed the cheap perfume on his dripping brow. 'If you say so, Kuznetsov. But let's hope that Cossack bastard on the hill is equally aware of the power of Bolshevism over Cossack steel and cunning.'

'*Comrade General!*' His Chief of Staff said, shocked.

But Kozlov wasn't listening. Already he was applying more powder to his broad ugly face so that he could present a more or less cheerful look to his staff. With Alexei defending the vital height, he needed it.

Outside the barrage began to die away. Zero hour was not far off now.

A signal flare hissed into the sky. Standing next to the General behind the first antitank gun screen covering the road, Gregor tensed. This was it.

Red lights blazed suddenly through the yellow haze. White blobs flew towards them, gaining speed at every moment.

'Solid shot, Cossacks,' Alexei roared above the row. 'Quite harmless, unless one of them hits you in the eggs. But they're coming up with tanks, stand by everybody!'

Behind the guns, the hastily scraped together crews of veterans of the Red Army and frightened wide-eyed boys who had been pressed into service as ammunition carriers, tensed. Hastily the gun layers pressed their eyes to the rubber sights, while behind them the gun commanders raised their right arms, ready for the order to fire.

The clatter of rusty tracks and the squeak of shaking armour grew louder. Although the approaching tanks were still concealed by the yellow smoke, Alexei knew they couldn't be more than a couple of hundred metres away. The sweat started to trickle coldly down the small of his back. The roar of their motors was overpowering now. The last armour-piercing shell fired by the unseen tanks slammed against a stone wall behind them. Splinters flew everywhere. Alexei ducked. At that moment the first, low-slung T-34 emerged from the fog of war, its long barrelled gun swinging from side to side, as it sought its prey.

'*Fire!*' Alexei yelled.

The gun commander of the nearest A/T gun slapped his hand down on the layer's shoulder. The 50 mm erupted. A long vicious tongue of red flame snaked from its muzzle. Its wheels bounced high on the cobbles and the gleaming yellow, smoking shell case went clattering to the ground.

The T-34 stopped, as if it had run into a brick wall. Its front reared up, as the 30-ton tank lurched violently back on its rear sprockets. A second later black oily smoke started to pour from its turret and four smoking, fear-crazed men were trying to clamber out of it to be mown down ruthlessly by the Cossacks' machine guns.

The T-34s were streaming out of the yellow smoke everywhere, their machine guns chattering. Alexei swiftly surveyed the tanks. Then he spotted what he was looking for — the command tank.

'That's our pigeon,' he roared to the gun commander nearest him. 'As usual in the Red Army, the radio signalling equipment has broken down. Look at him waving his flags like a lad at a parade. Pop him off and the rest of them are as blind as bats. They won't know what to do next.' He dropped his hand on the young Cossack's shoulder, quite calm although the tanks seemed to be be almost on top of them now. 'Get me that fat pigeon will you, lad.'

The long antitank gun swung round. The gun layer's dirty fingers spun the range wheel frantically. He pressed his eye against the rubber of the sight. '*On!*' he yelled.

'*In!*' the loader screamed, as the breech lever shot up.

The gun layer tensed. The command tank was only three hundred metres away now, its commander still waving his little flags furiously, as he ordered his tanks into the V-attack formation. He took a deep breath. '*Fire!*' he bellowed.

The antitank gun reared up on its twin trails. Automatically the crew flung open their mouths so that their eardrums wouldn't burst as the blast shot back. A long tongue of scarlet flame hissed from the muzzle. The solid shot — all six pounds of it — hurtled towards its target like a bat out of hell. At that range they couldn't miss. The command tank spun back like a wild horse being saddled for the first time. Its turret rocked violently. Desperately, but in vain, the commander grabbed for a hold. The turret in violet flame. In an instant his overalls were a mass of greedy flames. Screaming frantically he dropped from the turret and writhed on the ground in a desperate attempt to put out the fire. He sprang to his feet, the flames mounting ever higher and ran blindly into one of his own tanks. He flung up his charred claws in one last scream of agony before disappearing beneath its churning metal tracks.

All was confusion. The T-34s lumbered forward blindly in uncoordinated individual attacks to be destroyed easily by the massed antitank guns lining the road, while Alexei muttered, 'Typical Red Army. Once the command goes, the young buggers don't know what to do!'

Ten minutes later it was all over. The survivors were firing their smoke dischargers and attempting to conceal their withdrawal in clouds of thick white smoke. But the smoke could not hide the six wrecked or burning hulks that they were leaving behind nor the charred remains of their still burning comrades spread out over the scorched steppe.

'All right ... all right!' Alexei was forced to yell in the end, trying to calm his excited amateur gunners. 'Cease fire, will you! That's only the start. They'll be back for more. You'll need every single round you've got before this day is over. Cease fire!'

He had just taken a mighty swig of cold tea and vodka from the pail that one of the older men from the barracks was passing round the gunners when Peter von Kranz came galloping up the shell-littered road, crying urgently, 'General ... General, you must come at once. The Reds are attacking with infantry to the south...'

CHAPTER 2

The Cossacks watched amazed as the élite infantry formed up on either side of the gleaming white road, dressing their long ranks as if they were going on parade, rather than into battle, shuffling their gleaming top boots in the dust, shaven heads under their helmets set rigidly to the left as they took up their dressing.

Their commander, an emaciated giant, brought down his gleaming sabre. Very faintly, they could hear his command. One thousand young heads swung to their front in rigid unison. Then there was silence as the officer cadets waited in the burning midday sun.

Slowly Alexei lowered his glasses. 'Officer-cadets — Stalin's scholars,' he announced sadly. '*Komsomol* to the man... Eager to die for the glorious Soviet Fatherland and little Father Stalin.'

'And we're the boys who are going to help them on their way,' Gregor grinned wickedly, flashing a look along the line of Cossack riflemen and machine gunners dug in on both sides of the road. 'Let them come. We'll show them how to die for that Georgian bastard!'

Ahead of them, there was a sudden movement. The little group around Alexei quickly raised their binoculars and focused them on the Stalin Scholars. They saw a flash of sunlight on silver and gold. Smaller men with the broad epaulettes of bandsmen were forming up in the centre of the road between the two lines of rigid infantry. 'Well, I'll piss in my boots,' Viktor exploded in German, using the infantryman's phrase, 'they've even brought up the band! What a country!'

A moment or two later the band was in position. The emaciated commander of the Stalin Scholars swung round stiffly on his heel, his gleaming sabre resting on his right shoulder. He was too far away for the watchers to understand his words, but they could guess what they were: 'The glory and honour of dying for Mother Russia — and all the rest of the lies that commanders have always told young men,' Alexei said softly.

The commander turned. He raised his sabre. A hoarse command. The dull boom of the big drum. A sparkle of silver as the band raised their instruments before breaking into a lively military march. As one, the Stalin Scholars started to advance, bayonets tucked under their right arms, as if they were on parade in the Red Square for October Revolution celebrations, goose-stepping past Stalin himself.

A thousand metres ... nine hundred ... eight. The Stalin Scholars advanced in perfect formation, their gleaming high boots throwing up rhythmic clouds of dust as they stamped them up and down to the silver, spine-chilling music of the band.

'My God,' Viktor breathed, his voice full of disbelief, 'have you ever seen anything like it, Peter?'

His companion, gaze glued on the advancing formation, shook his head. 'No ... Viktor, something like this could only happen in Russia.'

They were five hundred metres away now. Already the waiting Cossacks in the trenches were curling their sticky, sweaty fingers around the triggers of their weapons, their lips suddenly very dry, their hearts racing with tension, apprehension and the hot desire to kill.

Four hundred and fifty.

The music stopped. '*Battalion — battalion, halt!*' cried the skinny giant.

A thousand feet crashed to a halt. Slowly the white dust settled down. Alexei raised his binoculars and with them swept the ranks of their pale faces.

'Battalion — battalion, dress!'

With a rapid shuffling of feet, the Stalin Scholars took up their dressing once more. Peter shook his head in disbelief. Armies hadn't fought battles like this since the days of Frederick the Great and his 'Long Giants', armed with muskets with a range of no more than one hundred metres. Satisfied with the cadets' dressing, the commander raised his sabre and bellowed: 'Battalion — battalion, prepare to charge. *Charge!*'

'*Hurrah!*' the hoarse cry went up from a thousand young throats. They broke into a clumsy run as one, following their commander, his sabre gleaming in the sun as he directed its tip in the direction of the waiting Cossacks.

'*Fire!*' Alexei yelled.

All along the line the machine guns burst into hysterical life. The advancing Stalin Scholars ran into the angry lead, as if into a solid wall. Within ten minutes the first rank had disappeared as if it had never even existed, swept away by the ruthless Cossack fire.

But the next rank came on, trampling over their dead and dying comrades, yelling their desperate hurrahs, following their lone commander to their deaths.

The Cossacks fired again and again. Already the barrels of their machine guns were glowing a dull red with the sheer volume of the fire, and here and there Cossacks were ripping open their flies and sluicing the barrels with their own urine in a desperate attempt to cool the guns off before they seized up altogether. Still Stalin's élite came on, great gaps in their ranks now. At their head, the commander tottered onwards, his smashed sabre held in a hand which dripped with blood, his once immaculate uniform ripped to pieces by Cossack bullets.

Two hundred metres ... one hundred and fifty... Their ranks growing ever thinner. One hundred metres. Now they were a handful of crazed survivors, some of them hopping after the rest on shattered legs or even crawling, their guts trailing behind them.

In the end Alexei could bear the slaughter no longer. 'In the name of God,' he yelled above the crackle of small arms fire, '*finish the poor bastards off.*' Sickened beyond all measure by the terrible slaughter of the youthful idealists, he drew his sabre and before anyone could stop him he was running down the slope towards the bloody survivors, swinging his sabre to left and right His Cossacks abandoned their weapons. Obscenities pouring from froth-flecked lips, they rushed after their commander like a pack of wild animals to fling themselves on the Stalin Scholars, slashing, hacking, slicing. It was over in a matter of minutes. As the Cossacks sank to the ground, sabres gleaming crimson in the sun's rays, their breath sobbing, the survivors fled back the way they had come, leaving the steppe littered with the dead of the broken regiment.

Gregor, slumped on the burnt grass with dead cadets all around him, raised his sweat lathered face and gasped: 'General, we've broken them... Broken the élite.'

Alexei nodded. But he did not speak. For the first time since the Cossacks had started their trek westwards, he realised just how foolishly wasteful war was. With a sigh, he thrust his sword into the earth to wipe the blood off, then slid it into its scabbard. 'All right,' he commanded, his voice normal once more, 'back to your positions everybody — and quick! They'll be here again soon.'

That night while the guns rumbled south and north, softening up the Cossack positions for another attack, Alexei took stock of their situation, while in the corner of the cellar which had become his HQ on the Tartar Hill, Peter and Viktor attempted to raise their own people.

All afternoon the Cossacks had been subjected to heavy artillery and two — fortunately highly inaccurate — dive-bombing attacks by a squadron of Stormoviks. A little later, cautious Soviet patrols had begun to nibble at his perimeter defences, searching for weak points on the Cossack line. Alexei tugged at the end of his nose thoughtfully and stared at a young Cossack lying propped up against the wall, calmly sucking his clay pipe, although his leg had been shot off and the blood was pouring through the paper and rag bandages packed around his gaping wound. 'Poor young bugger,' he muttered to himself.

All the signs indicated that on the morrow the Red Army would launch a properly coordinated attack. There would be no more easy targets for the Cossacks like the Guards Tankers and the Stalin Scholars. This time, the attack would be planned properly.

He frowned. Time was running out. Tomorrow he might have to give up the road if his men suffered too many casualties. He would never give up Tartar Hill, the key position. But where were the Fritzes? That was the most important question.

He looked across at the German Major crouched over the Afu set. 'Well?'

Peter von Kranz raised his earphones for an instant and shook his head. 'Impossible to get a fix, General. The air's absolutely crowded with traffic. Obviously the coming offensive —' he broke suddenly and his eyes lit up.

'What is it?'

Peter concentrated on the faint metallic stream of rapid morse. It was Tresckow's HQ all right!

He started to rap out Alexei's plea for help to the man at the other end. 'STILL HOLDING OUT ... ROAD AND BARRACKS STILL IN OUR HANDS ... STOPPED TWO ATTACKS THIS DAY ... EXPECT FURTHER ATTACKS IN THE MORNING ... CAN'T HOLD OUT MUCH LONGER ... CASUALTIES HEAVY ... EXPEDITE ... EXPEDITE RELIEF ... *OVER.*'

Nothing happened. Peter rapped out his call sign furiously again and again, the beads of sweat standing out on his brow. But the traffic which heralded the coming German offensive was too heavy and in the end he had to give up, his shoulders bowed in defeat. Taking off his earphones, he whispered: 'Sorry, General, I simply can't get through again. Let's hope they got the message and act accordingly.'

CHAPTER 3

'Comrade General,' the whining voice said at the other end of the phone, 'this is Aleksandr Poskrebyshev speaking.'

Kozlov gulped. With his free hand he dabbed cologne on his forehead, feeling himself break out in a cold sweat at the very mention of the name. He had met Stalin's sinister hunchbacked secretary only once, but that had been enough to put the fear of God into him. Get on the wrong side of that man, he had told himself at the Kremlin when Klementy Efremovitch Voroshilov had introduced him to the man, and you might as well get yourself fitted for a wooden overcoat there and then. 'Yes, Comrade Secretary,' he heard himself saying, while all around his staff tensed apprehensively.

'Comrade Stalin would like to have a small word with you about the situation on your front, Comrade General. That is if you've got time from your duties?' purred the unctuous voice.

'Yes,' the General forced himself to say. 'I've got a few minutes free just at present.' The General's big hand holding the receiver was wet with perspiration.

'Stalin here,' the voice was clear and pleasant, but marred for Kozlov, who came from Moscow, by the strong Georgian accent, which sounded so foreign. 'Is that you, Kozlov?'

'Yes Comrade Stalin. Good evening.'

'What is this shit I hear about your front, Kozlov?'

'How do you mean, Comrade?'

'I hear from Nikita Sergeyevitch that you are having some trouble down there?' the voice was still soft, pleasant.

Kozlov could feel the sweat pouring from his body. At that moment he could imagine 'Old Leather Face', as the Army called Stalin behind his back, hunched over his usual glass of pepper vodka, his dark, pock-marked face set in the look of contempt that it always seemed to bear when he spoke to his generals.

Kozlov licked his lips uncertainly, hoping that God would come to his rescue and knowing that he wouldn't. 'Well, Comrade Stalin, it seems that —'

'*Seems*,' Stalin interrupted. 'What are you — a Yid schoolmaster in some shitty rabbi school or a Soviet general? Make up your mind, man — what is it?'

'Sorry, Comrade,' Kozlov said hastily. 'Well, we're having some trouble in our rear area.'

'What kind of trouble?' Stalin's voice was under control again, but the menace was still there.

'A group of Cossacks — Don Cossacks — have occupied a stretch of the road to Novorossiysk...' His words trailed away helplessly, his mind full of those cruel old fox's eyes which had sent thousands, hundreds of thousands to their death, waiting for the inevitable explosion of rage.

'I see,' Stalin said mildly enough. 'Now listen to me very carefully, Comrade General. This spring has been a very bad one for my commanders. A lot of them who have failed me have suffered serious accidents, you understand me? Indeed I have asked Lavrenti Pavlovich to look into the matter.' He paused and Kozlov could imagine him sucking at the big curved working man's pipe which he still smoked to impress the man in the street that he led a simple way of life, although the truth was that he lived in incredible luxury and excess. 'I am sure that you understand me fully, Comrade General?'

'Yes Comrade,' Kozlov said unhappily.

'Then move your shitty kulak arse and wipe those damned Cossack traitors off the face of the earth tomorrow morning,' the dictator roared in sudden fury. 'If you don't let God protect you from my wrath!'

Lieutenant-General Kozlov was not the only military man who was braving the wrath of a dictator that particular evening. After the unsuccessful morning's conference with von Manstein, Colonel von Tresckow had made a decision: he would not let Operation Cossack be ruined because of the stubbornness of some hidebound commander. He had phoned von Kluge and told him what he intended to do. Naturally 'Clever Hans' declined all responsibility; he was not going to risk Hitler's anger. But he did allow his Chief of Staff to borrow his own private Fiesler Storch. One hour later the Colonel was flying south to the 'Wolf's Lair' to make a plea for aid to the 'greatest captain of all times', as the Army cynically called Hitler behind his back. Now he was waiting in the senior officers' lounge, furnished with spartan simplicity, hoping that the laughing officers and golden pheasants sitting at the wooden stools drinking their evening schnapps would soon become aware of his presence.

They were all there, the gang around Hitler. Himmler, his skinny frame clad in the field-grey of an SS general, his hollow chest devoid of any decorations save the Sports Medal. Martin Bormann, dressed in the dark brown of the Storm Troops, looking like a boxer gone to seed with his gross belly. Keitel, field marshal and the gang's chief today, sitting ramrod straight as ever, a wooden grin on his wooden face. Pudgy 'Professor' Hoffman, who had made a fortune as the exclusive purveyor of Hitler's photographs to the German public and who had introduced the Führer to his latest mistress, Eva Braun. The only missing member of the gang was Jodl, the brains of the HQ, and Hitler's Chief of Staff.

Despite his anxiety and haste, Colonel Tresckow could not conceal his contempt of the men with whom Hitler surrounded himself. All of them were hopelessly compromised and corrupt. The one with his string of mistresses, the other with his mysterious attempts to grab more and more power behind the Führer's back, perhaps even aiming for leadership of the German people himself. He breathed out hard. One day, he promised himself, when the Army had won the war, there would have to be a reckoning with these swine.

At last Keitel deigned to take notice of him. 'Well, Colonel, why aren't you at the front?' he rapped harshly. 'What do you want here?'

Colonel von Tresckow clicked his heels together and reported in the approved fashion, addressing the massive Field Marshal in the old-fashioned, indirect form, knowing that it would flatter Keitel's colossal ego, and then added: 'I have a request to make to the Führer, sir.'

'What did you say, Tresckow?' Himmler said, putting down the glass of white wine with which he had been toying. Bormann looked at the plump officer with bored interest. 'What is this?'

'It is in connection with Operation Cossack, Reichsführer,' the Colonel said, aware suddenly of the mess he had landed himself in now. 'You remember?'

'What is this — Operation Cossack, Heinrich?' Bormann asked, rubbing a drop of schnapps from his pugnacious boxer's chin.

Himmler explained hesitantly, while Bormann's face grew darker. 'But Heinrich,' he exclaimed. 'How the devil could you have involved yourself in such a crazy scheme. *Cossacks! Um Himmelswillen*, you know what the Führer thinks of the Slavs?'

'But Martin, I was only trying to contribute to the success of our operations in the south,' Himmler protested unhappily, a thin flush spreading over his pale face.

'Heinrich,' Bormann did not attempt to conceal his contempt for the Head of the SS, 'although we are at war, we cannot compromise our National Socialist principles. The Slavs are sub-human, little better than hewers of wood and drawers of water for our German folk comrades.' He puffed out his fat chest importantly. 'We Germans have no need of any aid from such an inferior race.'

'Yes, yes, Reichsleiter,' Keitel agreed forcefully, as always seizing upon any opportunity to toady to the Führer's Secretary and the most important man in the Reich after the Führer himself. 'How right you are.'

'Of course I'm right,' Bormann snapped, rising to his feet, his gross belly bulging unpleasantly under his stained brown shirt. 'I am a Mecklenburger, and we Mecklenburgers know about the Slavs. Our forefathers put the toes of their boots up their dirty Russki arses and kicked them beyond the Oder.' He laughed coarsely. 'And a thousand years later that's all they're still good for, to carry out German orders and have the toe of an honest German boot applied to their nasty backsides if they don't move quick enough.' He directed his menacing gaze at von Tresckow. 'You — what's your name?'

'Von Tresckow, Reichsleiter,' he answered, scarcely able to conceal his disdain for the gross, drunken golden pheasant, who was risking the whole of Germany's future because of some absurd racial theory.

'Well then, *mein lieber Herr Oberst*, you'd better get back to where you belong — the front — and start planning how you'll win your battle with good German blood. We don't need the help of some half-wild Cossack cowboys.' Waving a hand in a gesture of careless dismissal, he belched so hard that he had to sit down.

The Colonel looked at Himmler appealingly.

But the Reichsführer chose to ignore him. He swung round and began toying with his glass of white wine again, while Field Marshal Keitel, Germany's senior soldier, toady to the end, started to refill the company's glasses.

The Colonel waited stubbornly.

At the table, pudgy 'Professor' Hoffman broke the sudden silence by reaching into his pocket and pulling out a handful of photographs. 'Did you ever see these, gentlemen?' he asked. 'Now these are calculated to give even Fat Hermann a stiff one.'

There was a chuckle at the reference to Hermann Göring's supposed impotence, as Hoffmann began passing them round, starting with Bormann, who had a great collection of pornographic photographs himself.

In the end Colonel von Tresckow gave up. Sadly, he turned and while the gang of them drooled over the pictures, he went out into the night, cursing Hitler and the whole bunch at his headquarters, knowing that now General Alexei's fate was sealed.

CHAPTER 4

The sky was flushed with the light of the dawn sun.

As it hung poised on the horizon, the Stormoviks dived in like a flock of black hawks. For a moment they hovered above the road and Tartar Hill, while down below the alarms sounded urgently. Then the leader jiggled his wings and the divebombing attack began. Below in the rubble of the barracks, Alexei, squatting next to the rest, tensed, hands pressed tightly over his ears. The day was starting as yesterday had ended — in blood.

The leader dived with its engine roaring and its sirens howling hideously. Behind it the rest of the flight peeled off one by one. At five hundred kilometres an hour, the three planes dropped out of the harsh blue sky, black shapes hurtling — or so it seemed — to their destruction. Somewhere a lone Cossack gunner sent a stream of red and white tracer zigzagging towards them.

Just as it seemed that the leader must crash headlong into the ground, he levelled off, his engine screaming, the plane shuddering violently. A myriad black steel eggs wobbled awkwardly from its dove-grey belly. To left and right the other two Stormoviks shuddered to a halt a mere two hundred metres above the steppe, and discharged their bombs too. For one brief moment, there was a thick silence, broken only by the whine of the bombs hurtling down on the Cossacks cowering at the bottom of their holes.

The first stick exploded with an ear-splitting crash. Alexei felt the ground rise and smash into his face. Something hot, wet and salty streamed from his nose. His own blood. All around him glass splinters, followed by fist-sized, red-hot metal ones, hissed through the air. A wave of hot air struck Alexei in the face. His lungs felt as if they must burst and he gasped for air. Everywhere Cossacks were screaming for help. But there was no help forthcoming. Those who were still uninjured were burrowing deeper into their holes, as the whole weight of the Soviet dive-bombing attack descended upon them in remorseless cruelty.

Time and time again, they came in for the attack, hurtling in from the burning sun, machine guns spitting vicious purple flame, bombs streaming from their bellies. One Stormovik pilot, carried away by the heady excitement of his attack and the lack of danger, failed to pull out of his dive in time. At five hundred kilometres an hour he plunged into the steppe, shattering into a million pieces, snuffed out like some gigantic candle.

But the fate of their comrade did not deter the rest. They came in for one last attack, the three flights spread out like the prongs of an enormous Cossack hay fork, stark black and menacing against the blue wash of the sky. Bombs swamped the top of Tartar Hill.

'*Down*,' screamed Alexei madly, as the world rocked wildly all around him and the whirling gale of metallic death swamped them.

There were dead and dying Cossacks everywhere. Alexei staggered groggily to his feet and stared around at their crumpled bodies in the uncanny hush that followed the air attack. A boy was slumped under a heavy beam, his legs raised slightly, one hand placed under his head as if he were asleep, save for one thing — his young body had been severed neatly into two halves. A jumbled mass of twisted weapons and limbs settled slowly into a pool of congealing blood. A body minus a head stood on the cobbles, complete with fur cap. A fat old Cossack, propped up against a shattered wall, stared at the guts sprawling from his ripped-open belly into the bloodied dust. And above it all Alexei could hear the sound of someone screaming, like an animal caught in a trap.

But there was no time for the wounded, for already the bugles were sounding their shrill warnings on the road below and someone in the courtyard was hammering the iron alarm triangle, crying '*Alarm, Alarm*! To arms, brothers!'

Alexei picked up the rifle he had taken from a dead cadet and blew the dust from the bolt. Next to him, Peter von Kranz called to his fellow German, who still crouched there fearfully.

'Viktor, for Chrissake, man, they're coming!'

Viktor did not move.

'Are you hit?' Peter called in alarm.

From the road below came the first snap and crackle of the fire fight. The Red artillery would be joining in soon. Viktor did not answer, but remained there, his head buried in his dirty dust-covered hands.

Peter pulled at his shoulder angrily. 'What the hell's the matter?' he roared.

'I can tell you,' Alexei yelled, brushing past the two Germans. 'He's got his heart in his britches, as we say! He's simply shit-scared.'

Peter von Kranz looked down at his fellow agent, his dark eyes wild and full of horror. 'Come on — didn't you hear, the Ivans are on us any minute!'

'I can't go ... I've had enough,' Viktor muttered. He tried to wrench his shoulder free from Peter's grasp.

'Man, you've got to get up!' Peter hissed through savagely clenched teeth. 'You are a German officer, you must set an example to the Cossacks.'

'I can't.'

Peter hesitated for a second then whipped his pistol across Viktor's ashen face from left to right. It snapped back and Viktor's head slammed into a fallen beam behind him. 'You'll fight, you black bastard — you'll fight all right,' Peter bellowed, beside himself with rage. 'Now get on your shitty feet, before I put an end to your miserable life here and now.' He cocked his pistol to show he meant business.

The SS officer shook his bloody head, as if he were suddenly waking up. Without another word, he rose to his feet and accepted the Schmeisser machine pistol that Peter thrust angrily into his hands. 'Now come on,' Peter commanded in a harsh voice, 'let's get mobile!'

Viktor Teufel obediently followed the one-armed blond giant, his fear replaced by a look of hatred in his slanting Tartar eyes. He promised himself that one day he would blast a bullet into the broad inviting back that ran in front of him.

'*Siberians*,' Alexei commented grimly, as he crouched with Gregor in the forward observation post, watching the undersized soldiers in their earth coloured blouses push steadily forward up the road, rolling up strongpoint after strongpoint. 'Siberians, as cruel and remorseless as the Japanese themselves.' Alexei spat angrily into the hot dust and focused his glasses on the group of little men busily engaged in slitting the throats of their Cossack prisoners.

Kozlov's infantry had been attacking all morning. Wave after wave of them, thrown in by their anxious commander with reckless abandon so that their lifeless bodies covered the steppe as far as the eye could see. Alexei had finally stopped the Red attack to the north. But the fresh Siberian infantry to the south were a different proposition. They disdained the frontal attacks of the normal Soviet infantryman. Their approach was more subtle: small groups of lightly armed skirmishers, seeking out the weak points in the defenders' positions, followed by a swift, all-out rush of well-spaced and bold special assault troops who had been supplied with liberal doses of their favourite fermented mare's milk and drugs before they attacked.

The squat little men from the East had reduced the Cossacks' perimeter to about three hundred metres of road and a depth of fifty metres on both sides, plus the barracks on the top of Tartar Hill, its walls steadily crumbling away under the persistent Soviet artillery fire from both sides. For the moment, however, the Siberians had stopped their relentless pressure, resting obviously on their laurels, dealing with the prisoners in their own cruel Oriental fashion and waiting for reinforcements to come up so that they would have the necessary muscle for their final attack on the Cossack positions.

'What are you going to do, General?' Gregor asked anxiously, rolling carefully on to his back and staring up at Alexei.

'*Do*! What Cossacks have always done when the situation has been hopeless. Attack, Gregor — attack!'

The plan was put together swiftly as they crouched there under the leaden sky, no sound audible now save the persistent thud-thud, followed by the earthshaking roar, of the long-range Soviet cannon pounding the fortress above them on the hill.

'Your Siberian, you must remember,' Alexei lectured them, 'is much tougher than the average Russian stubble-hopper of an infantryman. But he has one weakness. He is a creature of habit and rules, admittedly his own rules. Now what does a sensible man do at this time of day in such heat?'

Gregor, the blood from the wound on his cheek dried black, attempted a worn grin. 'He takes a bottle of vodka, grabs himself a good woman and gets out of the sun and into bed — very smartish, General.'

Alexei smiled thinly. 'Of course, you get out of the sun — that is if you are a sensible man, who knows how to conserve his energy, and not some fool of an Occidental, who thinks he has to fight all day long. Look!' He pointed at the Siberians' positions.

The earth coloured infantrymen were burying themselves into the shade of their newly gained positions, thrusting out the Cossack dead on to the shattered parapets for extra protection, as if the dead men were so many logs of wood.

'So what will they do now?' Alexei continued. 'They will sleep until they are ordered to attack again by their commanders, which will naturally be when the heat of the day has vanished. So what are we foolish Cossacks going to do while they are having their naps?'

'Attack,' Gregor said delightedly.

'But General,' Peter von Kranz protested, 'even if they postpone their advance until evening, they'll still have sentries out. With the amount of ground under your control at the moment, they'd spot you as soon as you made your first move.'

'I agree,' replied Alexei easily. 'Except for one thing.'

'Oh?'

'We are riding out under a certain talisman, which will confuse the sentries long enough to make them uncertain whether they should wait with their fire until they have consulted their sleeping officers: gentlemen — the white flag of surrender.'

One by one the riders sprang over the shell hole which barred the sole remaining exit from the barracks on the top of Tartar Hill and lined up in the shelter of the wall, their pistols and sabres concealed under the saddle blankets. Alexei felt the bag of earth round his neck and snapped at Gregor: 'Flag!'

The Cossack next to Gregor raised the pole surmounted by a pair of tattered, bloodstained drawers ripped off one of the raped 'field mattresses', now cowering virtually naked among the dying Cossacks in the cellar.

'All right, Alexei said easily. 'At the walk — advance.'

He guided his tired white stallion out of the exit into the bright gleam of the noon sun, followed by the rest, feeling very naked as they appeared in full view of the Siberian infantry. Their chatter died away in sudden apprehension. There was no sound save that of their horses' hooves and the soft clatter of their metal equipment.

For a few minutes their movements were hidden from the Siberian sentries by a little gully, then they were in the open again, their tired mounts picking their way delicately over the pitted, holed, shell torn ground. 'Extended order,' Alexei ordered softly, 'Pass it on Gregor. But make it nice and easy. Nothing deliberate.'

Slowly the Cossacks started to spread out, while Alexei's hand sought and found the pistol he had hidden under the blanket

One hundred metres ahead of them, the first of the Siberian sentries sprang out of a shell hole. Crouching slightly on his bow-legs, he raised his round barrelled tommy gun.

'Standfast!' Alexei hissed between tight lips.

They rode on, but still the Siberian did not fire. More and more of the Red infantry started clambering out of their holes, many of them without their caps and boots, as if they had been disturbed in their sleep. They were a mere fifty metres away now. A taller Siberian, sabre dangling at his side, came into view, his metallic blue-black hair tousled, his face flushed, as if he were angry at being roused from his sleep. He gazed at the advancing Cossacks in open-mouthed amazement. They were thirty metres away from the Cossacks now.

At last the Siberian officer reacted. He opened his mouth to shout an order. Gregor whipped out his pistol and fired at point-blank range.

'Throw away those dirty drawers!' Alexei yelled, as the first wild shots burst from the surprised Siberians. Raising himself high in the stirrups, he pulled out his own automatic and fired a burst at them. Then tossing it away, he drew his sabre and cried, 'Cossacks —*charge!*'

Sabres flashed. Pistols barked. The Siberians, caught completely by surprise reeled back. Within seconds the Cossacks were through the enemy's first line.

A group of officers attempted to make a stand around a command post, kneeling in the white dust and firing erratic bursts of wild, panicky machine pistol fire at the Cossacks galloping towards them. Alexei's white stallion faltered and fell to its knees as it was struck a glancing blow by a slug. Alexei tugged at the bit viciously. In a second it was up again and plunging forward with the rest, the blood streaming down its white flank.

The officers' resistance melted away. As Alexei hacked at their bare shaven heads they reeled to all sides, trampled under the horses' stamping hooves. Not one of them survived the wild charge.

The Siberians were throwing their weapons away everywhere, fleeing the way they had come, fighting each other in their panic-stricken efforts to escape from the bearded butchers on horseback.

'Halt — *halt.*' Alexei gasped at last, reining in his sweat lathered, bleeding mount and letting his bloody sabre droop at his side. 'They've had enough.' He breathed out hard, and gratefully accepted the bottle of vodka which Gregor had snatched up from one of the dead officers as he had ridden by. He poured a stream of the fiery liquid down his parched throat. Then he wiped his lips with the back of his hand which was smeared to the wrist with Siberian blood. 'Well, that showed the buggers that we Cossacks are even more cunning than they are, lads, eh —'

But in fact Alexei knew that he had no time to rest on his laurels. The Stavka would already be screaming for a counter-attack to recover the lost ground. The bombers would probably already be on their way.

What reserves were left to the Cossacks were hurriedly brought up (mostly lightly wounded men) and told to dig in before the Stormoviks reappeared. A couple of the Siberian light guns were swung round and positioned along the road so that at least one hundred metres of it could be dominated by the Cossacks. Rations were stripped from the dead bodies sprawled everywhere and flung into the slit trenches for the long night ahead.

Finally as the black specks on the horizon to the east indicated that the dive-bombers were returning in a hurry,

Alexei was satisfied that he had done all he could. Raising his voice, he cried hoarsely to the men in the holes, 'Just one more night, my Cossacks, that is all I ask from you... Tomorrow the Fritzes come, I promise you. *Tomorrow.*'

And then, followed by the pathetic handful of riders still left to him, he galloped hell-for-leather for the cover of the ruined barracks, while the infantry dropped into their holes as the first of the bombs started to whistle from the sky.

CHAPTER 5

Colonel von Tresckow looked anxiously at the luminous dial of his watch. The glowing green hands pointed to two o'clock. All around him the infantry and sappers of the 46th Infantry Division were pushing their assault boats into the still water, the slight noise they made covered by the roar of the initial barrage further north inland. 'What is your forecast, Captain?' he asked the burly Bavarian officer standing next to him watching his men pushing off from the shore.

The Bavarian, who was in charge of the landing behind the Soviet front on the Isthmus ('Manstein's trick'), shrugged slightly. 'I can't rightly say, Colonel. My stubble-hoppers are a good bunch of lads. Most of them have been with me ever since the start of this do. We should make the road by zero four hundred is my guess. It all depends then on how long those asparagus shifters of the Second Panzer take to link up with us for the drive on the Rampart.'

'By dawn then?' the plump, red-faced Colonel queried anxiously, wondering whether it was worth worrying by now about the Cossack General and Peter von Kranz.

The Bavarian, anti-Prussian like most of his countrymen, and made bold by the fact that he was going behind the front of a whole Soviet army with a mere four companies under his command, laughed cynically. 'Well, Colonel, if you still like to believe in fairies, you can kid yourself that we'll make the Rampart by dawn.'

'All right,' von Tresckow cried exasperatedly, his nerves running away with him after the tensions of the last twenty-four hours, 'when, Captain?'

'When?' the Bavarian repeated, pausing before he stepped into his own boat, 'that my dear Colonel von Tresckow has been dropped fairly and squarely into the lap of the God of War — like a piece of very hot shit. *Servus.*'

A moment later his boat was already out to sea, bobbing up and down on the waves. Like some primordial clap of thunder the German heavy guns behind the shore opened fire, colouring a brilliant orange the figure of the lone man standing there.

But the Bavarian's assault companies had more luck than he had anticipated. The Lieutenant from the Kriegsmarine who had volunteered to lead them in, found the precise spot where the first Soviet antitank ditch ran into the sea. While the Red gunners in their pillboxes poured a steady stream of steel at the Germans attempting to cross the causeway in a frontal attack, the Bavarian's boats sailed up the broad antitank ditch completely unnoticed.

Swift as arrows, the noise of their outboard motors drowned by the crazy noise of the barrage, they sped to both banks. As soon as they hit land, the infantry leapt out, firing from the hip until the surprised Russians started surrendering.

The battle hardened Bavarian had no time for prisoners. 'Shoot the Red bastards,' he ordered in this thick Munich accent. 'We haven't the time to drag their Ivan arses with us.'

'Kill the Popovs!' the NCOs roared at their men, their faces glazed with sweat in the light of the flares hissing into the inky sky along the front.

The veterans of the 46th needed no urging. Like so many of the infantry who had survived the murderous campaign in Russia, they had become completely brutalised by the last ten months. For them the Russians were little better than animals.

Almost without thinking, they turned their machine pistols on the wretched prisoners, mowing them down where they stood and clambering afterwards over the mound of their smoking, still twitching bodies, as if they were moving across a pile of logs.

By three that May morning, the Bavarian and his men had reached the vital coastal road, one hour earlier than he had anticipated. Now a Russian pillbox barred any further progress, but that didn't particularly worry the Bavarian. The young Lieutenant from the Kriegsmarine, who had steered them in, had confided to him before the landing that he hoped he'd win the Iron Cross for this operation, his first time in action. Now he called the boy over to him. 'Now Moses,' he said, 'would you like to win the big piece of tin?'

'Yes, sir.'

'Right then.' The Bavarian unslung the satchel full of stick grenades he carried over his broad shoulder. 'Crawl up to that Popov pillbox, whip the pin out of one of these grenades, stick it through the nearest aperture — and duck yer head smartish, if you don't want to lose your turnip.'

The Lieutenant seized the satchel eagerly, as if it contained all the treasures of this world. 'Thank you, Captain,' he cried excitedly, 'and Heil Hitler!' In the first ugly light of dawn, the Bavarian could see the fanatical gleam in his blue eyes.

'Yeah, Heil Hitler,' he answered cynically. 'All right, Moses, on your way.'

Five minutes later, the pillbox disappeared in a flash of angry flame. But the Lieutenant did not come back. 'Forgot to keep his stupid sailor boy turnip down, Captain,' an unshaven sergeant reported thickly.

'Remind me to recommend him for the War Service Cross, third class — posthumously,' the Bavarian grunted. 'All right, don't stand there. Get your crappy stubble-hopped arses moving! Let's get on with this holy crusade against the Bolshevik beast, eh.'

By four o'clock the advance infantry of the 46th Division were in complete control of the stretch of coastal road assigned to them by their commander, well dug in on both ends, with one company out in front, already probing its way down the road towards the dim outline of the Turkish Rampart in the far distance. But still the Mark IVs of the Second Panzer had not broken through the Russian front on the causeway.

Squatting in a ditch with the sergeant-major in charge of the reconnaissance company and several dead Russians, the Captain passed him a cigarette. 'Here, Sergeant-Major, have a cancer stick.'

'Not castrated, Captain, is it?' asked the NCO, using the soldiers' phrase for a filter tip.

'What do you think I am — a warm brother with my armpits shaven and frilly lace knickers under my field-grey?'

For a moment or two they crouched there smoking in silence and watching the angry stabs of flame, lighting up the heavy clouds of smoke over the south of the Rampart, where it ran down to the sea.

'What do you make of that firing up there, Captain?' the NCO asked, taking off his jackboot and rubbing his heel which was chafed red-raw.

'Put that damned dice-breaker of yours back on — God, the pong's making my guts do back-flips — and I'll tell you.'

'Sorry sir.' The NCO slipped his boot back over his naked foot.

'According to the currant-shitters on the staff at Div HQ, there's supposed to be some hairy-arsed Ivans up there, who've gone over to us and captured part of the Red line.'

The NCO flipped away the rest of his cigarette. '*Ach, du heiliger Strohsack*,' he exclaimed in surprise. 'Popovs fighting for us — what next!'

'Yeah,' the Captain agreed, as yet another giant shell slammed into the southern end of the Rampart. 'It's a funny old world, Sergeant-Major, that you can say again.'

'What are we going to do about it, sir?'

'Do?' the Bavarian officer pulled down the corner of his blood-shot red eye. 'Can you see any green there, Sergeant-Major?' He didn't wait for an answer. 'We're gonna sit down here until those asparagus Tarzans of the Second Panzer force us to get off our arses and do something. We've captured our objective and that's that.' He took a last contented draw at his cigarette and settled back against one of the dead Russians he was using as a back-rest. 'As far as Frau Muller's boy is concerned, the Ivans up there can fight out the rest of this crappy war between themselves.' He closed his eyes pleasurably. 'Wake me up, Sergeant-Major, when the Asparagus Tarzans arrive…'

On that same evening the barracks on the top of Tartar Hill had become a graveyard for the Cossacks. An hour before, they had lost the last of the road in their hands and the bombardment had ceased so that the squat Siberian infantrymen could assault the hill. Twice they had attacked and twice they had been beaten back, leaving the shell pitted slope littered with their dead.

Now the bombardment had begun once more while the Siberians regrouped. Shell after shell slammed into the smoke-covered summit, throwing up gigantic holes, pounding into the brickwork still standing, tossing up the already dead and the new dead indiscriminately. The *Katuska* rocket mortars roared like infuriated beasts. The dull groaning noise, unlike anything else in the world, grew in volume as they sped through the yellow smoke to explode in vicious fury like a swarm of enraged hornets.

Outside the slope stretched a lunar landscape, with the dead slumped across the barbed wire like bundles of shabby rags. Inside in the cellars, the wounded and dying were packed everywhere, with more being brought in every moment on doors used as stretchers, the stretcher-bearers stepping carelessly on the dead, too weary even to hear the ghastly groans which came from their heat bloated bellies as they did so. Already some of the shell-shocked, wounded younger men had broken. Taking the traditional Cossack way out, they had hooked their big toes round the triggers of their rifles lodged beneath their chins, and blasted themselves to eternity.

Now their shocked eyes were coated with a hot sheen, as if tears were close. Their hands trembled continually. Every time one of the gigantic shells slammed into the barracks, they jumped violently, their nerves almost gone.

But Alexei refused to give up. At this moment of supreme crisis, he was at his most superb. Dodging the fist-sized shrapnel which scythed through the air all the time, he was here, there and everywhere, encouraging, upbraiding, crying over and over again to the weary demoralised men in their holes: '*Hold on Cossacks — just a few minutes more and they'll be here to relieve us!*'

But the Germans did not come. The bombardment intensified until it had become a supernatural tumult, a stationary panorama of horrific sound, sighing, whimpering, shuddering, screaming, as the air was torn apart time and time again. And in their cellars and holes, the survivors buried their aching heads in their hands to escape that agonized passion of noise.

Thus it was, despite Alexei's vigilance, that the defenders did not hear the rusty rattle of the T-34s as they ground up the slope to the east, followed by trails of slow, wary infantrymen. Even when the bombardment had ceased suddenly and the enemy had penetrated into the courtyard itself the Cossacks were too benumbed by the volume of fire to be aware of the enemy's presence.

By the time they had realised, it was too late. In a matter of minutes, the fresh Siberian infantry had driven them in weary, panic-stricken flight into the cellars or up into the dead Commandant's big house, while below in the battle littered courtyard, the triumphant Reds went wild with delight at their easy victory.

Mattresses were ripped and tossed out of windows, as they searched for loot, feathers flying wildly as if it were snowing in the midst of that baking heat. Already a group of them, drinking out of bottles of captured vodka, were nailing a screaming young Cossack to a window sill. A metre or so away, a fat older Cossack lay sprawled on his back, while a drunken officer plunged his sabre repeatedly into his guts.

Alexei wiped the sweat off his streaming brow, as he crouched with some of the survivors in the top floor of the Commandant's house and stared down at the terrible scene below. It was like a teeming anthill, full of drunken, cursing Siberians, firing their submachine guns into the air in wild abandon.

'Holy Mother of God,' Gregor cursed, 'it's like a lunatic asylum down there!'

'What the hell are we going to do?' Viktor gasped. 'They're crazy — they don't know the meaning of surrender.'

'*Surrender*,' roared Alexei. 'Who's talking of surrender?' He swung round at the handful of Cossacks trapped with him in the top floor. 'Listen brothers, we can only die once, can't we?'

'Ay,' they answered in unison.

'Then let's try to give ourselves a chance. If we don't make it, then we'll die like Cossacks always have died — with their weapons in their hands.' He drew his sabre and looked at their worn, bloodstained faces, his harsh expression replaced by one of pride.

Peter stared at the Cossack General in frank admiration. In this moment of despair, Alexei alone still had the courage to hope, was still the supreme leader of men. No wonder his men trusted him.

'Gregor,' Alexei continued, 'get ready to open the door.'

'Peter,' Viktor whispered urgently, his face ashen and contorted. 'We are German officers. We won't —'

'*Halts Maul, duneiger Hund!*' Peter cried, beside himself with rage. 'Fight and die — that's what you're going to do now. And for God's sake, try to die like a man!'

'*Now!*' Alexei bellowed.

Gregor flung open the bullet-pocked door, then thrust himself through it, firing his submachine gun from the hip. The group of Siberians, tramping drunkenly up the steps, were bowled over in a flash, writhing, screaming, pleading as the merciless fire swept them down the stone flags. The Cossacks trampled over them as one, shrieking their fearful oaths of revenge. A young Siberian raised his head above the bloody carpet of his comrades' bodies. Alexei aimed a terrible kick at his bloody jaw.

They burst into the body littered square. The stupefied drunken Siberians panicked. They simply did not know where to run. One of the men, dressed for some reason in woman's clothes, tried to swing himself on to a Cossack horse. A dozen guns spoke and he smacked to the cobbles, a line of red holes perforating his back.

But already the Siberians were beginning to rally. Fresh troops were running up the slope, firing indiscriminately as they came, hitting both comrade and Cossack alike. One of them flung a grenade right into the centre of the group around Alexei. The General ducked in time. Viktor was too slow. He dropped like a stone, screaming in agony, the blood fountaining in thick jets from his severed right foot. He disappeared under the trampling feet just before Peter von Kranz could reach him.

A grenade exploded ten metres from Peter. With the kick of a mule, the blast struck Peter in the chest. He was lifted bodily into the air and dashed down again. The air was full of the smell of burning. 'Alexei,' he called, 'General…'

The Cossack Commander spun round. Peter von Kranz lay sprawled out on the bloody cobbles, the left side of his face a gory mess. Slowly he pointed a red smeared hand at something Alexei could not see; then the whites of his eyes rolled upwards and his head fell back. He was either unconscious or dead.

But Alexei had no time to concern himself with the one-armed German. A Siberian was running straight at him, face lathered in sweat, his long bayonet already tipped with Cossack blood. Alexei drew his pistol and fired but missed. The Siberian fired in his turn. Alexei felt a burning pain in his thigh and fell to one knee. The Siberian lunged. Desperately Alexei twisted himself to one side. The Siberian shot forward and overbalanced.

With all his remaining strength, Alexei dived on him. His nostrils were assailed by the man's rancid, heavy male smell. He writhed violently to free his right hand. Alexei could guess what he was after — his knife. But he didn't give the soldier a chance to get it out. Thrusting out one hand, he grabbed the Siberian's throat, hooked his fingers in the nostrils of the flat nose like the prongs of a fork — and tugged brutally.

The Siberian's shrill scream of pain was drowned by the twin streams of blood which flooded the cavities. Alexei grabbed his knife as it clattered to the cobbles. Before the Siberian could twist to one side, he had raised it and plunged it deep into his breast.

Blood was streaming down his leg from the wound in his thigh as Alexei rose to one knee. Ten metres away Gregor was screaming in his death agony as a sheet of dazzling flame from a phosphorus grenade devoured his writhing body and his panic-stricken hands clawed the air.

'Gregor,' Alexis called thickly. He staggered forward a few paces. At his feet he thought he saw a pistol, clasped in a hand inexplicably attached to no body. Painfully he bent in an attempt to pick it up. Somehow or other, he simply couldn't manage it. The red mist kept blotting out his vision.

He shook his head violently. His legs felt as if they were made of rubber. Yet somehow through it, he sensed voices other than Russian close by. A Siberian stumbled against him. He recognised him as an enemy only by his rancid odour. Blindly he lashed out and clamped his hands on the enemy's throat, the man's face a red, wavering blank. Surprisingly the Siberian made no attempt at resistance. He did not even gasp with pain, as Alexei exerted the last of his rapidly waning strength. The mist threatening to overcome him at any moment, Alexei pressed harder and harder, his sole remaining wish now to squeeze the life out of this unknown, unseen man before death overtook him.

Then from far away, a coarse Bavarian voice was crying in a language he only half understood, 'All right ... all right, you hairy-arsed Cossack, let go, will you?' Rough hands prised open his fingers round the Siberian's neck. 'The bastard's dead already... Let go, will yer?'

The 'Asparagus Tarzans' of the Second German Panzer Division had arrived.

THE UKRAINE, DECEMBER 1942

Outside the shabby collection of wooden huts which made up the Cossack Division's HQ in the Ukraine, an easterly wind was blowing icily over the snowbound steppe. In every direction it stretched bare, white and dead: empty save for a solitary black crow flying low over the white waste, dragging its harsh cry behind it in mournful despair.

Lieutenant-Colonel Peter von Kranz, astride his horse, shivered suddenly. The snow had conquered Russia once more. The good months were over. The bad time had come again, as if the very weather symbolised what lay ahead for the ten thousand Cossacks of the new division drawn up on the frozen square.

'What is it, Colonel?' asked Major Boris, Alexei's new Chief of Staff.

Peter von Kranz avoided looking at his lobster pink, hideously scarred face, the result of his T-34 being brewed up by a German antitank gun in 1941. 'Nothing, Major. A louse just ran over my liver, as we say in German.'

They fell silent, waiting for the General to appear. Over the radio from one of the huts came the sound of the insidious voice that had been haunting them for seven days now: '*Achtung, deutsche Kameraden*! Do you know at Stalingrad that a German soldier dies every six seconds? Think of it German comrades — every six seconds, one of your pals dies in the encircled city. For what, I ask you? *Stalingrad, comrades is a mass grave*!' Over and over, the Soviet speaker hammered home the terrible message.

Peter von Kranz was glad when someone switched the station over to the usual military band music that the *Deutschlandfunk* had played most of the day ever since Stalingrad and the half a million German soldiers who held it had been surrounded in a pathetic attempt to cheer up the worried nation. Pensively, he turned his attention to the Black Cossack Division. The only difference between their appearance and that of the ordinary German soldiers was their black fur *papenkas*.

There weren't many of the original Cossacks left in their field-grey ranks. The Battle of the Turkish Rampart, which had opened the way for Manstein's drive to Stalingrad, had taken its toll. The new Division had been formed from the Wehrmacht's prison camps, with shaven headed, horribly emaciated Red Army prisoners, who had rallied to General Alexei's black flag because they were Cossacks or because they didn't want to starve to death behind German barbed wire.

All summer and deep into the autumn, they had trained hard in this godforsaken part of the Ukraine, their presence kept secret at Himmler's express order. Now, once Himmler had inspected them, they would be flung into battle for the first time in an attempt to break through to Field Marshal von Paulus's Army trapped in Stalingrad.

Peter von Kranz sighed again sadly. Suddenly he felt very old. How long ago it seemed since he had set off with high hopes to rescue the General from the camp. Then he thought he might realise the heady dream of raising the flag of revolution throughout the Soviet Union. But that dream was long dead. The Soviets were winning and as General von Tresckow had told him wearily only a week ago: 'That fool of a Führer of ours won't tolerate the idea of a Russian sub-human bearing a German weapon!'

But if Colonel von Kranz despaired that icy morning, the commander of the Black Cossacks did not. As he put the last touches to his uniform, the tunic decorated now with the Iron Cross, First Class, which von Tresckow had wangled for him somehow or other, Alexei stared at his lean, darkly handsome face in the mirror and told himself that everything was not lost by a long chalk. Now he had the power of a whole Division in his hands, complete with artillery; now he could talk to the Fritzes on different terms. Besides they were in trouble — serious trouble in Stalingrad. It would only be a matter of time and they would come begging to people like himself. Their reserves were running out rapidly. All that would be left to them were the three million Red Army prisoners in their cages, who could form divisions, corps, whole armies of trained, experienced fighting men if called upon.

With his new Division he would show Himmler and the small-town fat-bellied grocers in uniform with whom he surrounded himself, what real soldiers were and when the time was opportune, it would be his turn to make the demands and the conditions. Satisfied with his appearance, he tilted his *Papenka* at a bold, rakish angle in the true Cossack fashion, and went out.

'Morning, Cossacks!' he cried, reining in his true white stallion and staring challengingly at their suddenly rigid ranks.

'Morning, General!' ten thousand hoarse throats echoed the greeting, their breath fogging the icy air, and ten thousand sabres gleamed in salute in the thin rays of the winter sun.

Colonel von Kranz and Major Boris stiffened in their saddles. Alexei, in high good humour at the prospect of going into action again, waved them to relax. 'Well, Colonel?' he asked Peter, 'where's this celebrated Reichsführer of yours? We march to the railhead at zero ten hundred hours, as you know.'

The Colonel glanced at the watch on his one hand. 'Ten minutes' time. Whatever else is wrong with the Reichsführer — and there's a lot — he's always punctual, General.'

Precisely ten minutes later, Himmler's little convoy arrived from his nearby Field HQ: two Mark IV tanks rumbling at the head of the four camouflaged staff cars, with a mobile 20 mm flak wagon bringing up the rear as protection against the Soviet partisans who were now flooding the rear areas.

'General, that's the Reichsführer, in the second Mercedes.'

Alexei smiled thinly. 'Your precious Reichsführer looks as if he's about to fill his britches at any minute. Does he think we Cossacks would tolerate any partisans in our area?'

A moment later Himmler and his entourage descended from their vehicles. Peter von Kranz spotted a badly limping Viktor behind Himmler, but he had no time to give his sudden appearance in their midst any thought, as Alexei commanded: 'Cossacks of the Black Cossack Division — general salute!'

Ten thousand sabres flashed as the Cossacks pressed the hilts to their lips in salute. Standing next to Viktor, Himmler paled, as if he feared the half-wild riders might suddenly decide to charge him at any moment. Weakly he raised his gloved hand to his cap in a gesture of thanks.

Alexei ordered the parade to rest and then with Colonel von Kranz as interpreter, he trotted over to the waiting Reichsführer and his staff who were staring curiously at this latest addition to the German Wehrmacht.

Alexei reined in his stallion and saluted. 'Reichsführer,' he began, staring down contemptuously at the pale head of the SS, whose pince-nez was already beginning to cloud over in the intense cold. 'We Cossacks have fought side by side with our German comrades for centuries. We fought for Wallenstein. We fought with you in your own War of Liberation and was it not our own Hetman Count Platov who liberated your own Berlin from the French in 1813?'

Peter von Kranz quickly translated Alexei's words (which he had helped to prepare himself, knowing Himmler's weakness for German history) but his eyes were set on Viktor's dark Tartar face which was cast in a sneer of contempt as if he knew whatever request the Cossack Leader had must fail right from the start.

'Reichsführer, the Cossacks are once again prepared to shed their blood for the German cause. But, in return, once the situation in Stalingrad is cleared up, we demand that you honour your promise to return us to the Don.'

'Demand!' Himmler exploded, his pale face flashing. Then he caught himself as if he had realised that his creation had independent life of its own. 'Tell him Viktor,' he rapped, 'that at this moment I cannot give such a guarantee. The Führer would have my head if I did. Indeed,' he added fussily, 'I am risking my whole political career now by secretly forming this division. Tell the Cossack that.'

Viktor translated his Chief's words, his dark eyes full of malice, making no attempt to soften the blow to Alexei's hopes.

'Tell him too, Obersturm,' Himmler continued, 'that as a token of my good will and continued interest in the Cossacks, I am attaching you to the General's Division as my personal representative on his staff.'

Alexei nodded when the Obersturmbannführer was finished.

'So we are to have our political commissar too,' he commented in a loud aside to von Kranz, who now realised why Viktor had turned up again, 'the SS is going red, I see.'

Viktor flushed angrily.

Alexei turned to Himmler again. 'Good then, Reichsführer,' he said, his lean, harsh face grim, his eyes cold, 'we shall play your mercenaries a little longer. But beware Himmler — *beware*! When the time comes, we shall sing another tune.' With that he swung his horse round, its tail flicking the Reichsführer's face.

Himmler's staff gasped at this deliberate insult to the most feared man in Europe. Alexei did not hear. Facing his men, he bellowed harshly: 'Black Division at an easy trot — *Forward*!'

He spun his white stallion round and digging his spurs into its sides, cantered forward, his icy gaze set firmly ahead. Himmler's staff backed hurriedly out of the way as the Cossack Division started advancing, fifty abreast, their rigid riders rising and falling rhythmically on their immaculately groomed mounts, their hooves kicking up tiny spurts of snow. As he watched them trot by at that moment, Peter von Kranz felt the tremendous primitive power of these half-wild men; then he too urged his horse forward to join their ranks. Their fate, whatever it would be in the uncertain years to come, would be his too.

At the head of his Cossacks, General Alexei Bogdan gave a sigh of relief, as the icy wind of the snowbound steppe cooled his angry face. Again he was free of the importunings of the Germans. He was on horseback and going into action once more, with ten thousand of his loyal Cossacks trotting behind him in a thundering avalanche of man and beast.

Suddenly the tall lean General, with the hard, scarred face rose high in his saddle and sucking in a great breath, cried harshly: 'Cossacks of the Black Division — *at the gallop*!'

He dug his spurs in the white stallion's flanks. The horse sprang forward, mane flying. Behind him, his Cossacks seized by the old Cossack furore, ducked their fur-capped heads low over their horses' outstretched necks, teeth bared, all fears, all doubts gone, as they galloped towards the distant horizon, where the bright flickering of the German opening barrage indicated that already the new battle was waiting for them.

A NOTE TO THE READER

Dear Reader,

If you have enjoyed this novel enough to leave a review on **Amazon** and **Goodreads**, then we would be truly grateful.

Sapere Books

Sapere Books is an exciting new publisher of brilliant fiction and popular history.

To find out more about our latest releases and our monthly bargain books visit our website: **saperebooks.com**

www.ingramcontent.com/pod-product-compliance
Lightning Source LLC
Chambersburg PA
CBHW060435180626
46817CB00007B/2823